Creatures

Daddy's Gone A-Hunting

Their voices and footsteps faded into the night as they went away, and Andy let his breath go in a dizzy rush. This was completely, unspeakably, impossibly *insane*! To be out here in the middle of the night, crouching behind a wall, soaked and freezing. And terri-fied half out of his wits, because he'd believed – he'd *really* believed – that his dad and his brother were enemies who were out to kill him! What sort of madness was this?

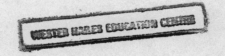

Creatures

Daddy's Gone A-Hunting

Louise Cooper

Hippo

Scholastic Children's Books
Commonwealth House, 1–19 New Oxford Street,
London WC1A 1NU, UK
London ~ New York ~ Toronto ~ Sydney ~ Auckland
Mexico City ~ New Delhi ~ Hong Kong

First published by Scholastic Ltd, 2000

ISBN 0 439 01205 8

Typeset by Falcon Oast Graphic Art
Printed by Cox & Wyman Ltd, Reading, Berks

10 9 8 7 6 5 4 3 2 1

1

"Dad," Andy Thorpe said, "what's the capital of—"

He didn't get any further, because Dad interrupted sharply, "*Shh!*" and leaned forward, pressing the volume button on the TV remote control. The early-evening local news was on, and the newscaster's voice swelled into the sitting room:

". . . no reports of any escaped animals. But this new sighting has re-awoken the old controversy between those who say the Fossewell Fiend can't possibly exist, and those who claim that it very definitely does."

The name "Fossewell" caught Andy's

attention, and he looked at the TV screen with sudden interest. A blonde-haired girl reporter, in wellies and waterproofs, was standing in the middle of the familiar village high street. She smiled professionally through the rain and went on, "Whatever the witnesses really saw, one thing *is* certain – the arguments and speculation will continue to rage. This is Kristie Kerr, for DalesData, in Fossewell."

The picture flicked back to the studio, and another newscaster started talking about health statistics. Dad thumped the mute button and flopped back in his chair again.

"That's all we need!" he said.

"What is, Dad?" Andy forgot his school work.

"Weren't you listening?" Dad demanded grumpily.

"Well, sort of, but only at the end." Andy paused, then added cautiously, "Were they say-ing . . . there's been another sighting?"

"They were!" Dad growled, and sighed in exasperation. "As if we didn't have enough to do, without this rubbish starting up again!"

He got out of his chair, switched the TV off and started towards the kitchen. Andy called after him, "What do they reckon they saw?"

Dad stopped in the doorway and gave him an annoyed look. "Frankenstein's Monster, for all I know or care! I'm too busy to waste time talking about things that don't even exist." He gestured angrily at the books and papers spread on the table. "And so should you be. Get on with your work, or Mum'll be home before you've finished."

He stomped out, and Andy sighed. When Dad was in this sort of mood there was no point even bothering to talk to him. It was always the same in spring; the farmers had loads of work, and when the weather was wet it made things even worse. Dad was as grouchy as a bull with a headache at the moment. Andy was almost glad that there was still a week to go before school broke up for Easter.

He tried to settle down to work again, but after a couple of minutes he realized that he wasn't concentrating. The news item – the bit of it he'd heard, anyway – was nagging away at the back of his mind, and it was much more interesting than a geography project. How long was it since the last sighting of the Fossewell Fiend? Last August, he thought, when a family of tourists reckoned some big, dark and alien-looking animal had dashed across the road in front of their car, and those smudgy tracks had been found up on the moor pastures. There'd been a terrific fuss about it at the time; the media had tried to blow it up into a huge story and the village had been inundated with tourists all hoping to see it. But there weren't any more sightings, and after a while the excitement had fizzled out.

Till now.

Dad didn't believe in the Fiend, and never had. He said, never mind tourists; if some wild animal *was* out on the moors, one of the farmers would have got a proper look at it by now. More to the point, they'd have shot it, and quite right too. Which was what he'd like to do to the sort of day-tripping gawpers who rampaged all over his fields, and dropped litter, and left gates open, and let their dogs run loose, frightening the sheep.

It was little wonder, really, that he was furious about the news item. Ordinary holiday visitors were welcome in the district, but the sort of crowds who came looking for a sens-ational story were another matter. It had been mayhem last year; you could hardly get into the village for people, and there were traffic jams in all the lanes.

Andy wondered if any of his school mates had heard the news and knew more than he did. He could phone a few of them and find out. . . But then he thought, if Dad came in and found him talking about it, he'd hit the roof. It was Monday tomorrow. He could see his friends then. It was safer.

Reluctantly, because tomorrow seemed a long way off and he'd lost any interest he might have had in geography, Andy went back to his work.

At school next morning, everyone was buzzing with the Fossewell Fiend story.

"It was on Saturday night," one of Andy's classmates said. "Someone was driving back from town, and it ran across the road in front of their car."

"They said it was like a big cat," someone else added, round-eyed. "Wish I'd seen it!"

"Nah!" a third person disagreed. "My dad's paper this morning says it was just a fox."

"It wasn't! It was too big."

"Well, a deer, then. Must've been!"

Pete Shaplock, who sat next to Andy in class, looked at him sidelong. "Bet *your* dad's hopping mad."

"Yeah, he is," Andy said ruefully. "He thinks it's all a load of rubbish, and it's just going to cause trouble."

"But what if it isn't rubbish?" Pete asked. "If it really *is* out there, people ought to know about it. I mean, it could be dangerous, couldn't it?"

"Do you believe it's out there?" Andy asked.

Pete shrugged. "Probably not. I reckon it was a big dog or something like that. Easy to make a mistake in the dark." His face broke into a broad grin. "Soon find out, won't we? If it kills someone – that'll get everybody's knickers in a twist!"

Good point, Andy thought. Not some*one* getting killed, of course, but some*thing* – a sheep or two, maybe. That hadn't happened last time, which was why interest had faded before very long. This time, though. . .

But there hadn't been any attacks yet, and escaped wild animals couldn't live on air. So on the whole he was inclined to agree with Dad, and Pete, that the whole thing was a lot of rubbish.

All the same, on the bus home he found himself peering intently at the passing country-side. He didn't expect to see anything strange, but he looked anyway. There was no sign of the Fiend. But as the bus rumbled along the lanes, a bright blue van, sprouting antennae and with DALES TELEVISION MOBILE UNIT painted on the side, overtook at about Mach 3 on the approach to a bend. The bus driver muttered about townie idiots who had no more sense than they were born with, and the van vanished over the crest of a hill.

Dad was in a much better mood when Andy got home, firstly because the rain had stopped, and secondly because he had some time to play with his new toy. His new toy was a tractor with all the latest whangdoodles on it, and when Andy walked into the farmyard he saw its nose poking from the open barn door, and Dad's feet sticking out from underneath it.

"Hi, Dad!" Andy pushed away Meg, the half-grown collie puppy, who came bounding to greet him. "Want any help?" He and his older brother, Martin, who had left school and now worked on the farm, liked messing around with the tractor almost as much as their dad did.

Mr Thorpe emerged and grinned through the oil smears on his face. "No – I was just checking a couple of things. Martin and I are taking a load of fodder to the sheep up near the Ridge later. Get your school work done, and you can come for the ride."

"Brilliant!" To Andy's mind there was nothing more exhilarating than riding high in the cab of the roaring, thrumming monster as it rumbled slowly and magnificently along the road.

"If Mum says so, mind."

"OK." He'd get round Mum. He always did.

Two hours later, with school gear changed for overalls, Andy scrambled up into the tractor's cab. There was just room for three, and he perched happily between Dad and Martin as with an enormous racket the tractor, with the big trailer in tow, juddered out of the yard and towards the lane.

"Won't be much traffic around at this time of day!" Dad yelled over the din. "So we won't cause a jam!"

"Want to bet?" Martin shouted back. "What about all the Fiend-spotters? Village was packed at lunchtime!"

Dad grinned. "Tough! We'll give 'em something *real* to look at!"

They turned out of the farm gate and started to rumble along the lane. The cab was so high that you got a fantastic view over the hedges and fields; from his perch Andy could see right across to the wilder moorland, a grey-green sea dotted with patches of bright yellow gorse. Flocks of sheep grazed over it, with lambs running among them, and in a nearer field was a small herd of cows. As the convoy passed by, the cows galloped away with their heads shaking and tails swinging. Andy smiled. You'd think they were used to tractors by now, but they always got in a flap when they saw one. Look at them, tearing around – and those sheep over there, they were as bad, and the tractor was nowhere near them!

Nowhere near them. . . ?

Andy frowned. Those sheep were *much* too far away to have been scared by anything in the lane. Something else had frightened them. Sightseers, he thought, and they'd let their dog loose. . .

He looked towards the area of the field that the sheep were running from.

What he saw was *not* a dog. All right, it was too far away to make out a lot of detail, but Andy had very good eyesight. Dogs weren't that big. They weren't that shape.

And no dog he'd *ever* seen moved in that

strange, fluid, *slinking* kind of way.

Andy's heart started to thump like the beat of the tractor's engine. His knuckles turned white as he clenched his fists, and his face was nearly as pale. He must be wrong, he told himself. He *had* to be wrong.

But deep down, he knew he wasn't.

His voice came out as a thin croak, as he gasped, "Dad. . ."

2

"Dad! Dad, LOOK!"

Andy found his voice properly and yelled at the top of his lungs. But Dad was negotiating a bend and only shouted back, "Can't – too busy!"

Martin had heard, though, and glanced over his shoulder. He saw his kid brother's face, and his grin vanished. "Andy? What's up?"

"Look!" Andy cried again, gesturing frantically. "Over there!"

The animal – whatever it was – was less than a hundred metres behind the running sheep, and closing. It moved smoothly and efficiently, its body low to the ground in a prowling, almost gliding motion. For a few moments Martin didn't see it, then suddenly his eyes widened.

"I don't believe it!" He grabbed Dad's shoulder. "Dad, stop! *Stop!*"

The tractor and trailer shuddered violently as Dad, startled, slammed on the brakes. "What the—" he flustered as they ground to a halt. "What's going on?"

Andy pointed across the field. "There's something chasing the sheep!"

"What? Where?" Dad craned. "I can't see it!"

"There, *look!*" Andy waved his arm wildly. But suddenly the creature wasn't there any more. The sheep were still scampering in panic, but the slinking shape behind them had vanished.

"It *was* there!" Andy's face was a picture of confusion, and he appealed to his brother. "Martin, you saw it, didn't you?"

Martin bit his lip. "I saw *something*," he said. "At least . . . I think I did. . ."

"And look at the sheep!" Andy persisted.

Dad frowned. "They're scared, all right. Something's up there – another blasted dog, it must be."

Andy shook his head. "No! It was the wrong

shape, and it didn't run like dogs do. It wasn't a dog. I *know* it wasn't!"

"Don't be daft, Andy," Martin put in. "Dad's right. What else could it have been?"

"If I had my shotgun. . ." Dad growled.

Martin shook his head. "No use, Dad. It's gone now." He scowled. "But I wouldn't mind taking a look up there tomorrow, to see if we can find any dog tracks."

Andy shook his head. "It wasn't a dog!"

They both looked at him, and Dad snapped, "Don't be so silly, Andrew!" He only ever used Andy's full name when he was annoyed with him. "Martin saw it too. Of course it was a dog." He glared at Andy. "And if I hear you saying anything different to anyone, you'll be in trouble, understand?"

"But—"

"*Understand?*"

Andy gave up. "Yes, Dad," he mumbled.

"Good. Because if the TV and papers get the idea that it's anything else, we'll have them swarming round Fossewell like wasps round a jampot."

"They're doing that already, Dad," Martin pointed out reasonably.

"Maybe they are," said Dad, "but that's no

13

reason to go making things even worse with wild stories. There was a dog stalking the sheep, and that's all there is to it. I don't suppose it'll come back, but if it does, we'll do something about it."

"What?" Andy asked uneasily.

"Shoot it, if necessary."

"Is that allowed?" Martin asked.

"Whether it is or isn't, I'll do it if I have to." Dad's face was grim. "I'm not having my sheep worried because some townie can't keep his precious pet under control!"

A horn sounded behind them at that moment. Andy looked over his shoulder. "Car," he said. "We're blocking the road."

A little yellow sports job had pulled up behind them. "All right." Dad started getting ready to move again, but before the tractor could judder into life, the car driver jumped out and came towards them. She was a youngish woman with blonde hair; Andy thought he recognized her face, but couldn't think where from.

"Evening," she said cheerfully. "Anything wrong?"

Martin grinned down at her. "No, thanks. Sorry to hold you up — we'll get moving now."

"Oh. Right." She looked at the tractor. "Lovely machine. Is it yours?"

"It is," said Dad. He sounded frosty, and Andy wondered why.

"Right, yeah." The woman smiled. "Must be great to drive. All that power." The smile broadened and she held up a hand. "I'm Kristie Kerr, from Dales Television. You might have seen me on the news?"

"We have." Dad didn't shake hands, and now Andy realized why he was scowling. Kristie Kerr was just about the last person in the world he wanted to meet. "Well," he went on, "if you'll excuse us. . ."

"Just a moment. I saw you were all looking over the fields, and pointing. Can I ask why?"

Oh, she had a reporter's nose, all right. Dad's scowl turned into a downright glare, and he retorted, "We were checking the sheep. But I don't suppose that's much of a news item, is it?"

"Ah. No." Kristie looked disappointed, but after a couple of seconds her professional smile came back. "Pity. I thought maybe you'd spotted the Fossewell Fiend, ha-ha!"

No one else laughed. Dad continued to glare, Martin looked away, and Andy stared at

15

a smear on the window as if it was the most interesting thing in the world.

At last Dad broke the silence. "There's a lay-by a bit further on," he said. "We'll pull in there so you can overtake."

He revved up the engine with a roar, so they didn't hear what Kristie said in reply. The tractor and trailer started to move, leaving the reporter standing in the middle of the lane and staring after them with a thoughtful look on her face.

It didn't matter what Dad said. The more he thought about it, the more Andy was sure in his bones that the creature running across the fields had not been a dog. What it actually was, was a question he couldn't answer. But that chance meeting with the reporter, Kristie Kerr, and her joky remark about the Fossewell Fiend, was getting to him. What if there really was something out there? An escaped wild animal, maybe. Or something even weirder. . .

At school the next morning he was bursting to tell everyone about what he'd seen, but he didn't dare. If Dad found out that he'd breathed a word to a living soul, he'd go completely ballistic. It wasn't worth the risk.

So, though it nearly drove him crazy with frustration, Andy kept quiet. By Thursday afternoon he'd resisted temptation for three whole days and was feeling more relaxed. Nothing else had happened, the press and TV were getting tired of the Fiend story, and tomorrow was the last day of term. So by the time school ended, he was feeling pretty good.

The feeling didn't last. Unusually, Dad's Land Rover was in the yard when Andy got home, parked at an angle, as if it had been left in a hurry. In the house, Andy found Dad, grim-faced, on the phone.

"That's the place," Dad was saying. "Two of them, yes. . . All right. Martin's already up there, so we'll see you in about half an hour. Thanks, Barry. Bye."

"What's going on, Dad?" Andy asked as Dad put the phone down.

Dad didn't waste words. "Martin found two dead lambs," he said. "Throats torn out, and half eaten."

"Oh, no! Where?"

"Up by the Ridge."

"But that's where—"

"Where you saw that dog on Monday. Yes, I know." Dad headed for the door and started to pull his wellingtons on. "Barry Bullen and Alf Stark are meeting us there. Tell Mum to expect us when she sees us."

Andy stared after the Land Rover as it swerved out of the yard. He thought about the dead sheep. About what might have killed them. Then suddenly he turned round and tore up to his room to change. He hadn't asked Dad if he could go along on the hunt, because he'd have said no. But Dad couldn't stop him from going out on his bike. And from the lane, about a mile away, there was a good view of the Ridge, where the dead lambs had been found. If anything strange *was* up there, it was the perfect place to look for it.

A couple of minutes later, with a pair of binoculars slung on his back, Andy pedalled away from the farm. The bike seat was too low for him to see properly over walls and hedges, and anyway, he had to use up all his concentration on the car drivers who seemed to think cyclists shouldn't, and therefore didn't, exist. After a while, though, the lane started to climb, and at last he stopped on the crest of the hill. Leaving his bike on the verge, he climbed on to the wide wall-top, took out the binoculars and scanned the rolling fields.

There were two Land Rovers in the distance, parked half-way up the Ridge. One was Dad's and the other, Andy thought, belonged to Alf Stark. But there was no sign of the hunting party, only the flock of sheep, so far away that even with the glasses they looked like cotton wool blobs. Andy guessed that Dad and the others were probably on the far side of the Ridge. There were trees over there, a likely place for a wild animal to hole up. For a moment Andy felt uneasy as he thought of Dad and Martin among those trees. Maybe the creature – whatever it was – was watching them. Maybe even stalking them, the way it had stalked the sheep. . .

He shook the unpleasant feeling away. Dad and the other farmers had guns, didn't they? And it wasn't as if the thing out there was the size of an elephant. It was probably as scared of them as they were of it.

All the same, he wished he could see some-one. Not knowing where they were, or what was happening, wasn't a pleasant sensation at all.

He watched for a few more minutes, but nothing happened. No one appeared, there was no sound of gunfire, and the sheep just went on peacefully grazing. At last Andy gave up. This was dumb as well as boring. He might as well go home.

He swung back on to the bike and set off, not hurrying. There was a long hill with a humpback bridge over a river at the bottom. The river was fringed with trees and bushes, but you could see the road clearly, and it was fun to coast down and do a wheelie over the bridge. Andy started down, picking up speed – then suddenly he glimpsed something in the riverside trees. Just a flicker of movement, but. . .

He braked, and slid to a stop on the bridge. It was very quiet. The only thing moving was the water in the river. But he was *sure* he had seen something.

He climbed off, moved cautiously to the bridge parapet, and peered over. And his pulse lurched.

There *was* a shape down there! Long and thin – it was in among the bushes and hard to spot, but he'd seen something twitch. Something that could have been a tail. . .

Very carefully now, and trying not to make any noise, Andy crept round the edge of the parapet and on to the sloping bank. Whatever it was hadn't noticed him yet. If he could just get a few metres closer. . .

Then, when he got half-way down, the shape wasn't there any more.

Andy stopped and stared, blinking. Where the heck had it gone? One moment he'd been looking at it, the next it had completely vanished! No animal he'd ever seen could move that fast or silently. It must have been a trick of the light. There wasn't anything there at all.

Excitement gave way to disappointment, and Andy started to climb back up the bank. It was steep, and slippery after all the rain, and suddenly he missed his footing and went slithering backwards. He was in among the bushes before he could stop himself, then his heel caught in a protruding root and he landed with a thump on his backside.

Muttering under his breath, Andy grabbed a branch to haul himself upright.

As his hand grasped it, something growled softly close by.

3

Andy froze, staring into the tangle of leaves and twigs. And his eyes bulged as he saw another pair of eyes staring back at him.

Behind the eyes a shape moved. Very slowly, very carefully, creeping fractionally nearer. It looked enormous, and Andy's whirling brain screamed silently at him to *run, get away, just RUN for it*! He couldn't. His legs were paralysed by shock and terror, and his teeth started to chatter uncontrollably.

"N-n-n-nh. . ." He was trying to say "No", trying to tell himself that this wasn't happening. But the word wouldn't come out. And the eyes – greeny-gold, with huge pupils – were still fixed on his face. *What was this creature?*

Then it growled again. This time there was real menace in the sound – and it broke the spell.

"*AAAH!*" Andy yelled in pure terror, and flung himself backwards, trying to scrabble up the bank. The eyes in front of him narrowed to emerald slits, and he had one horrifying glimpse of a mouth filled with lethal fangs as the growl became a savage snarl. The shape tensed, then crouched as if it was about to spring.

Above them on the road, a car engine revved and roared. The animal flinched – then it whirled round and was gone.

Andy didn't see it go. He was clawing his way wildly up the bank, scrambling, gasping, almost sobbing. He hadn't heard the car; all he could think of was getting away, getting to safety. His bike was on the verge and he flung himself astride it and hurtled away down the lane as if a herd of mad rhinos were after him.

The car was roaring away up the hill. It was a yellow sports car, and when the driver glanced in her mirror she saw Andy pedalling frantically away. She thought she'd seen him somewhere before. And she wondered what he'd been doing, and why he was in such a hurry.

Something else was watching Andy, too. It stared from the shelter of the riverside bushes until the bike was out of sight.

Then it glided swiftly, sleekly away along the bank.

Andy was shaking like a leaf when he got home. He dropped his bike in the yard, tore into the house and blurted the whole story out to Mum.

Mum was as horrified as he'd been. She dived to the phone straight away and rang Dad on his mobile. When she came back, her face was grim.

"They're going to go to the bridge to have a look," she told Andy. "I just hope they find it! If it had attacked you—" She shuddered. "I can't bear to think about it!"

Neither could Andy. He was still feeling shaken an hour later, when Dad and Martin came home. They hadn't found any sign of anything at the bridge, but Dad was absolutely certain that the thing that had menaced Andy was a rogue dog.

"It *wasn't* a dog!" Andy argued. "Dad, I *saw* it – it was only a metre away from me!"

"I know," said Dad. "But you were scared,

and it was in the bushes. You said you didn't see it clearly."

"No. . ."

"Then you can't know what it was for sure, can you?"

Martin chipped in. "Come on, Andy. Dad's right; it's got to be a dog. Some breeds can be pretty enormous, remember."

"And dangerous!" added Mum. "Think of the teeth on a Great Dane. Or one of those pit bull things."

"Exactly," said Martin. "Anyway, if anything really wild, like a big cat, had escaped from somewhere, the police would know about it, and they'd have warned us."

"What about the Fossewell Fiend, though?" Andy asked.

Dad snorted with furious disgust, and Martin sighed. "No one's really seen anything, have they? There's no evidence; it's all just rumours."

"And I don't want them spreading!" Dad warned. "Remember what I told you the other day? If we're going to sort this out properly, we don't want the press and TV hanging around." He gave another snort. "Or next thing we know, we'll have a bunch of do-gooders saying we mustn't shoot it and that we ought to feel sorry for it! So not a word to anyone, all right?"

Andy saw the logic of that, and nodded. "OK, Dad. I wouldn't have said anything, anyway."

"Good." Dad nodded firmly. "All right, then. We'll look for it again tomorrow. And when you go out on that bike, you just be careful, you hear me?"

Andy went up to his bedroom early, but he didn't feel much like sleeping. Instead, he sat by the window that overlooked the yard, thinking and worrying. Dad and Martin were both so sure that the mysterious animal was a dog, and now he was beginning to wonder if they were right after all. The idea of an escaped leopard or wolf or whatever was pretty farfetched. OK, the TV was making a big thing of the Fossewell Fiend, but that was their job, wasn't it? They wanted sensational stories. If they just said that a dog had attacked some sheep, no one except the farmers would be interested. So Dad and Martin had to be right, didn't they?

The trouble was, he couldn't quite make

himself believe that they were.

He thought about wild animals. Wolves. Leopards. Or even lions and tigers. What could creatures like that do to someone if they got angry – or hungry? Stories about people being eaten bubbled darkly in his mind. Eaten; and nothing ever found except a few bones. . .

But then, the lambs hadn't been eaten, had they? They'd just been killed, and that *did* sound more like a dog attack. Andy latched on to that thought as he tried to convince himself. It was a dog. It had to be. Anything scarier would have devoured its prey, like in the wild animal stories.

Unless, of course, something had disturbed it before it could eat. . .

That thought started him feeling nervous again, and his imagination ran riot. What if it *was* something else? When it got hungry again, it would kill again, wouldn't it? What if it was a person next time? What if it was Dad or Martin. . .?

He stared out of the window towards the fields and said through clenched teeth, "Whatever you are, I just hope they find you and shoot you quickly!" The fact that he was frightened of the creature made him hate it. It shouldn't be doing this to them. It shouldn't be allowed to.

His door opened suddenly, and Mum appeared.

"Not in bed yet?" she said.

"I'm just going." Andy moved away from the window.

"Yes, well, you try and have a good night's sleep. And don't forget Fiona's arriving tomorrow."

Andy looked at her blankly. "What?"

"Fiona – your cousin. Honestly, Andy, you've got a memory like a sieve! I told you; she's coming to us for the Easter holidays."

Andy's face fell like melting treacle and he groaned. "Oh, no! Not *her*!"

"What d'you mean, 'not her'?" said Mum. "You haven't even seen each other since you were both about seven!"

"I know, but she hated my guts then, and I hated hers!" Andy flopped sullenly on his bed. "Why's she coming here now?"

"Because your Uncle Colin and Aunt Chris are working in South America for six months."

"Oh. Well, she goes to some snooty boarding school down south, doesn't she? Why can't she stay there for the holidays?"

"Don't be so mean and silly, Andy!" Mum rebuked him. "I don't suppose she likes boarding school any more than you would, but with her mum and dad away so much, she has to go. She'll probably be feeling lonely and fed up, so I want you to be nice to her. All right?"

Andy scowled, remembering a loud-mouthed, bossy brat who'd boasted the whole time about how many expensive toys she had. And then she'd kept pinching his without asking, and had broken half of them. . .

"Andy. . ." Mum's voice was getting dangerous.

Andy let out a huge, resigned sigh. "All right, Mum," he said. "I'll be nice."

When Andy did get into bed, he couldn't sleep. First there was the depressing thought of Cousin Fiona. And when he managed to forget about that, his mind started to whirl around the subject of the mystery animal all over again. Lurking fears and crazy theories were still ping-ponging around in his head at midnight. But by half past, his brain was so tired that he couldn't think straight any more. *At last!* he thought. *Maybe I can get to sleep now*. He ought to turn the light off, really. But it was too much bother to reach out from under the duvet. . .

He fell asleep with the light on and one leg dangling over the side of the bed. And soon he started to dream.

He was walking slowly across one of Dad's fields – slowly because he didn't seem able to go any faster unless he started running. He didn't want to run; it seemed like too much hard work. So he plodded on, not knowing why he was here but unable to think of anything better to do.

There was something wrong with his eyesight, too. He couldn't explain it to himself, but it was almost as if he could see too much – the world looked wider than it should have done, like peering through a fish-eye lens. On one side he could see all the way across to the lane, while on the other he could make out the sharp rise of the Ridge. That shouldn't have been possible, but though he kept shaking his head to make the view come right, it wouldn't. And the ground looked a lot closer than usual.

He was still worrying about it, and getting more and more annoyed, when at one edge of his distorted vision he saw something moving.

Andy stopped and stood very still. The shape was dark, and it looked quite large. It was moving slowly in his direction, and at first he wondered if it was a sheepdog. He knew the sheepdogs. He didn't like them, but he wasn't scared of them, not really. But then he realized that it wasn't a dog. In fact, he'd never seen anything quite like it before.

Then, so suddenly that he jumped, a gust of wind blew, and the smell hit him.

It was like being punched in the stomach. A sensation of blind terror erupted in Andy, and it blotted out everything except an overwhelming urge to flee.

He swung round and ran – and the dark shape started to run as well. *It was coming after him!* One panicky glance behind showed it streaking in his direction, and Andy's legs pumped desperately as he tried to gather speed. But something was wrong with his legs, too. He couldn't sprint the way he usually did; instead, he was lurching clumsily over the ground. What was the matter with him? Why wasn't he moving faster? Why did his legs feel as if they belonged to someone else? The thing was gaining on him, and its horrifying scent was getting stronger every second! He had to escape before it caught up with him and – and –

Suddenly, in the distance ahead, he saw a familiar shape: a big object, trundling slowly along the lane beyond the stone wall. Dad's new tractor! Part of him (though he didn't know why) was nearly as scared of the tractor as of the pursuing creature, but another, saner part told him that where the tractor went, Dad went too.

Andy opened his mouth, and with all the power in his lungs yelled, "*DAD!*"

Or meant to. But what came out was a despairing, "*BAA-A-A-A-A!*"

The world around him jolted, and light flared in front of his eyes. There was something in the light – a shape rushing to meet him. . .

And a loud BANG echoed in Andy's ears as his skull slammed against the solid ground.

4

Andy raised his head groggily, and blinked in the glare of a lamp. He was sprawled on the floor, wedged between his bed and the table, with the duvet on top of him and one leg sticking up at a crazy angle. And his head hurt.

It took him a while to work out what had happened. The shock of waking up from the dream must have made him thrash around, and he'd fallen out of bed and whanged his head on the table edge. Gingerly, he fingered his skull. No blood, but when he pressed his left temple the pain made him wince. Concussion? Nah. Just a bruise, more likely. If it still hurt in the morning, he'd tell Mum. But he'd probably be fine by then.

Unsteadily, Andy retrieved the duvet and climbed back into bed. His heart was jumping under his ribs like a grasshopper in a jam-jar, and it wasn't helped by the fact that his memory of the dream was coming back. What an awful nightmare! To dream he was a sheep, and the Fossewell Fiend was chasing him – it made him realize how the lambs must have felt before. . .

No, he told himself, *don't even think about that!* His head still hurt, and he wondered if it really was concussion. Maybe he ought to get an aspirin from the bathroom. It might help him feel better.

He started to get out of bed again – and paused, frowning, as from outside came a clatter, as if something had been knocked over.

Andy's bedroom overlooked the yard and the barns, and his first thought was that Dad was still up and about. Then he looked at his clock, and that idea vanished. It was three in the morning; Dad wouldn't be in the yard at this hour.

Not unless something was wrong.

Andy went to the window. There was a gap in the curtains, and he put one eye to it, peering cautiously through. No lights out there, and no sign of anything moving. Anyway, if there was an intruder or a fox about, the dogs would be barking by now, wouldn't they? He must have imagined the noise. Or maybe it was an hallucination, after that bash on the head.

He rubbed his skull again and started to draw back from the window.

Then stopped, as he heard the second noise.

It wasn't a clatter this time. It was much softer – a sort of low, throaty cough, almost like someone clearing his throat.

Andy stood very still, ears straining, holding his breath. Then, with a suddenness that made his spine tingle, the sound came again.

It was right under his window.

His heart bounced in his chest, and it took all the nerve he possessed to inch forward and peer through the gap in the curtains a second time. For a moment or two he thought there was just empty darkness out there, but then a reflection showed in the chink of light spilling out from his room. *Two* reflections, quite small, and just a few centimetres apart.

From the yard, in the pitch-black of the

moonless night, a pair of alien eyes glared up at him with ferocious intensity.

And, softly, something *snarled*.

Andy couldn't move. He wanted to – oh, he *wanted* to, with every scrap of his will. But, just like the first time, his muscles had locked solid and he was completely frozen. The thing out there was motionless, too. It just *glared*.

Somewhere in his mind a voice was scrabbling to be heard. *Why aren't the dogs barking? They must have sensed it! Dad, Mum – wake up! Why don't you wake UP?* But his voice was as frozen as the rest of him; he couldn't yell for help. All he could do was stare, hypnotized, at the glowing eyes below him in the yard.

Eyes that burned into him like fire. . .

An eerie, prickling sensation began to crawl into Andy's brain. He couldn't see any shape behind the eyes; it was much too dark. But the thing out there was looking at him with a horrible awareness. It wasn't like being stared at by an animal. The creature – whatever it was – was observing him. Summing him up. *Thinking.*

Suddenly the pain in his head came back so ferociously that he gasped. The familiar shapes of the bedroom warped and twisted, and for a shocking moment everything looked *wrong*. It was all out of proportion, like the landscape in his nightmare – his vision was blurring, and he felt as if another mind was mixing itself up with his. A mind that was angry, and menacing, and *hungry* – and – and –

Without any warning, the glowing eyes blinked, and the spell that gripped Andy was broken. He jumped – and the creature outside moved, too. Andy glimpsed a flowing shadow, a glint of what looked like dark-spotted fur in the gleam from his window, and a low, sleek shape skimmed away across the yard.

As it went, the spell shattered completely and Andy yelled at the top of his voice: "*DAD! DA-A-AD!*"

There was a commotion on the other side of the wall, and as Andy raced out to the landing he met Dad, Mum and Martin piling out of their bedrooms.

"Andy?"

"What is it? What's the matter?"

Before they could all bombard him with questions, Andy gasped, "I saw it again! *It's in the yard!*"

Dad said, "*What?*" and Martin demanded,

"Did you see it properly this time? What did it look like?" Andy gabbled out a description – and Dad's expression changed.

"Glowing eyes?" he echoed, and Andy heard disbelief in his voice. "*Spots?*"

Martin snorted. "Sounds like something out of *The Jungle Book*! You must have dreamed it!"

"It was there!" Andy protested. "It was, honest!"

"Now listen, love," said Mum soothingly, "you had a bad fright when you saw that dog today, so it's not surprising if you had a nightmare about it."

"I did, but—"

"Well, there you are, then. If there really was something in the yard, the sheepdogs would have barked, wouldn't they?"

"Yes, but—"

"Come on," said Dad, sounding as if he was trying hard not to feel annoyed. "It was just a dream, Andy. Go back to bed, and try not to wake the whole house up again, hmm? I need my sleep, even if—"

He didn't get any further because at that moment an explosion of noise – squawking, clucking and screeching – burst from the hen-house on the other side of the big barn. Downstairs, adding to the cacophony, the two grown sheepdogs and Meg the puppy all started to bark and yelp hysterically.

"Good grief!" Dad jumped as if he'd had an electric shock. "Martin – *quick*!"

He and Martin pounded downstairs. Andy, running after them, was in time to see Dad snatching his shotgun from its secure cupboard while Martin flung open the back door. All three dogs streaked out and Dad and Martin raced after them, barefoot and in their pyjamas. Dad was loading the gun as he went, while Martin swung a powerful flashlamp across the yard. Andy wanted to follow them, but when he got to the door his nerve failed. After what had happened at the bridge, he was too scared.

The dogs' barking was more distant now, and the din from the hen-house sounded like World War Three. Then, cutting shockingly through the chaos, came two loud, sharp *bangs*.

As the sound of the shots rang out, Andy almost screamed. For one single moment the pain in his head had come back with a vengeance, and with it a stab of pure terror that he couldn't explain. The kitchen walls seemed to leap up and out, as if he'd tripped over and fallen on the floor – then as suddenly as they had come, the pain and the fear flicked away, and everything was normal again.

Except that, inexplicably, he felt *hungry*.

Breathless, Andy clutched the edge of the table to steady himself. Luckily Mum hadn't noticed; she was staring tensely out of the back door. Andy tried to get a grip on his nerves, and was just starting to recover when Dad came hurrying back towards the house with the shotgun in his hand.

"I missed it!" he said breathlessly. "It's gone – ran away towards the fields. That thing's fast!"

"What was it?" Mum asked urgently. "Did you see?"

Dad shook his head. "Not properly. Just got a glimpse. But it was too big to be a fox."

"The dog, do you think?" she said. "The same one that killed the lambs?"

"I'd bet anything on it," said Dad.

Andy thought: *No, Dad, no! This time I did see it, and it ISN'T a dog!* But he didn't say it. There was no point.

"What about the chickens?" said Mum. "Did it kill any?"

"I saw one dead one, but I don't know if it got any more," Dad told her. "Martin's checking now."

"I'll go and help him, and calm them down." The chickens were Mum's territory and she knew best how to deal with them. She put a coat on and hurried outside, and Dad turned to Andy.

"You were right, Andy," he said grimly. "Good job you woke us up, or it would have done much more damage before we got there. Well done."

"It got away, though," said Andy.

"This time, yes. But don't worry – we'll get it. Sooner or later, we'll get it."

He went to put the shotgun away. Andy watched . . . then something in his head lurched. The room swam momentarily, and a queasy feeling washed over him. For an instant, the fear had come back. And something else, that he couldn't explain. Something that started a worm of doubt writhing in his mind.

No! he told himself fiercely. *You got a scare, that's all. There's nothing weird going on.*

That creature might be ferocious, but it's only an animal.

Isn't it. . .?

5

There were two dead chickens in the hen-house, and another two missing. The low door where the birds went in and out of their run had been torn off its hinges, and there was a hole in the surrounding wire big enough for Andy to have crawled through.

But something more than the raid was bugging Andy – and bugging him in a big way. His memory was a bit muddled, but two things stood out clearly. First, the feeling he'd had as he stood hypnotized at the window had been very different from what he'd experienced at the bridge. All right, he'd just had a bang on the head, so maybe he'd been a bit woozy.

(He still had a headache this morning, and a whopping bruise was coming up.) But he'd *felt* that creature's thoughts as clearly as if they were in his own head. Somehow, it had reached out to him, projecting its thoughts with a spooky kind of telepathy. For a moment he had known what it was like to *be* the Fossewell Fiend. And it had terrified him.

Then there was the one glimpse he'd had of it as it bounded away, before it broke into the hen-house. A long, lithe body and a spotted coat. What type of animals had spots? The only thing he could think of was a leopard. But leopards were quite small, weren't they? The thing in the yard – and the thing he'd encountered in the bushes – had been *big*. More like the size of the lion or tiger that he'd been worrying about.

So what was it?

Two mysteries. And then Andy remembered a third – the fact that the dogs had kept quiet until the chickens started squawking. That was weird, too. Dogs have very sharp ears, and a terrific sense of smell. They *must* have sensed the intruder! So why hadn't they barked earlier? It was almost as if it hadn't been a real animal out there, but something. . .

Supernatural. . .?

Andy wanted some answers, and he wanted them badly. The trouble was, he didn't even know where to start looking.

Martin picked Cousin Fiona up from the station at noon. Andy was in his room, and when he heard them arrive in the yard, he looked out of the window. Martin was lugging a suitcase out of the Land Rover, and as Mum emerged from the house, Fiona got out.

Andy would never have recognized her. She was still tall and skinny, but her long fair hair had been cut short, and she was wearing trendy clothes and even trendier glasses. She had "townie" written all over her, and Andy's spirits sank into his feet. Oh, great! If his mates got one look at her, he'd never live it down!

Moments later the dreaded summons came.

"Andy! Come downstairs!"

Andy thought of six excuses not to, realized that Mum wouldn't believe any of them, and reluctantly went.

Fiona was standing in the kitchen. She grinned at him, and Mum, with a don't-be-rude-or-I'll-murder-you warning look, said, "You remember Fiona, don't you, Andy?"

45

"Yes," said Andy dismally. "Er – hi."

"Hi, Andy." Fiona's grin became wider. "I just bet you remember me! I busted most of your toys last time, didn't I?"

Andy said, "Yeah," and looked away, and there was an awkward silence. Then Mum, sounding artificially jolly, said, "Well, Fiona love, I expect you're hungry, so we'll have lunch early. I'll get it started while Andy shows you your room."

"Thanks, Auntie Jo," said Fiona. She waited, and at last Andy realized what he was supposed to do.

"Through here," he said, picking up the case and jerking a thumb towards the hall and the stairs. "And mind the first step; it's steeper than the rest."

"I remember."

They trooped upstairs and along the landing to the spare bedroom. Andy opened the door, and Fiona stood on the threshold for a few moments. Then she said, "Wow!"

"Wow. . .?" Andy echoed cautiously.

"Yeah. This is *fabulous*! And all to myself! I have to share with three other girls at school." She walked into the room and started touching things. Then suddenly she stopped and turned to look at him.

"Sorry about the toys," she said.

Andy blinked, and she laughed. "OK, I know it was yonks ago, but I bet you still hate me. That's all right, I hated you then, too. I thought you were a snotty-nosed little creep. *And* you were a boy – yeuch!" She pantomimed putting her fingers down her own throat.

Andy couldn't help it; he burst out laughing, too, and Fiona gave an exaggerated sigh of relief. "Whew! Well, we've got that bit out of the way at least!" She grabbed the case from him and dumped it on the bed. "Oh, by the way, Fiona's got to be one of the dumbest names going. I hate it, specially when the teachers at school say it." She pulled a face and put on a la-di-dah voice. "Fyer-NAH! So call me Fiz, all right?"

"Fiz. . .?"

"F-I-Z. It's not brilliant, but it'll do. So: here I am, then, and you're stuck with me all the holidays."

"That's OK." Andy was beginning to change his mind about Fiz. Well, people grew up, didn't they? At least she had a sense of humour. And if she swapped those clothes for something more sensible, they might even start to get on. He felt a bit sorry for her, too. It must be awful to be stuck in a boarding school and then have to spend the holidays with relations you hardly knew, because your parents were always travelling on business.

Oh, well. Maybe he could do his bit to help her have some fun while she was here. If nothing else, it'd get his mind off the Fossewell Fiend.

"S'pose I'd better get unpacked," Fiz said suddenly. "Where's the bathroom? I've forgotten."

"Oh – turn left, and it's the door at the end," Andy told her. "I'll leave you to it, then."

"Yeah. Thanks." She paused, then smiled again. "This is a great house. You're lucky, living here."

Andy beamed. She was OK.

"Hey," he said. "Just a thought. . . Do you like tractors?"

By the end of her first evening, Fiz was settling in as if she'd lived at the farm all her life. She'd explored the yard and the barns, her room was already a mess, and even Dad had given up trying to call her Fiona. She wasn't interested in tractors, but then you couldn't have everything. On the whole, she *was* OK.

At supper she ate like a horse. In fact, Andy thought, she'd probably have *eaten* a horse if there'd been one on her plate. She did make one blunder at the meal, when she asked Dad brightly about the Fossewell Fiend. She'd overheard some people talking about it on the train, and she was curious. Dad spluttered in his food, and Mum said tactfully that it really was a lot of silly nonsense, and she mustn't worry about it. Later, Andy heard Mum having a quiet word with Fiz in the kitchen. The words "chickens" and "rogue dog" were mentioned, so he guessed that Fiz had been given the standard story. He didn't interfere. Better not to.

Andy's head was aching again when he went to bed. He'd brushed his hair over the bruise so that it didn't show, but now he wondered if he should have told Mum about it. Maybe he *had* done himself a serious injury, and if he ignored it it'd turn into a brain tumour or something. . .

Oh, shut up! He was as bad as Dad's dippy Aunt Polly, who kept deciding she had some new killer disease! Turning over crossly, Andy pulled the duvet up around his ears and shut his eyes. *Count sheep,* he told himself. He started to picture a whole flock of sheep jumping over a gate. One . . . two . . . three . . . four. . . This was *boring*. Good. Maybe it'd work, then. Five . . . six. . .

HUNGRY!

Andy shot bolt upright in bed as the feeling hit him out of nowhere. It only lasted for an instant, but it was so powerful – a huge, ravenous hunger; a craving to hunt, to chase, to *kill*!

"Uh-*ah!*" He clutched at his stomach, doubling over and convinced for one awful moment that he was going to throw up. He didn't; the sickness vanished as quickly as the hunger had done, and within a few seconds everything was back to normal.

Except that Andy felt as if his mind had been invaded.

6

Over the next two days, Dad, Martin and several of the other local farmers went looking for the animal. They found no sign of it. But on the second day, to Dad's annoyance, they ran into Kristie Kerr again. She was with a TV crew, filming a Fiend report (though there wasn't much to say) for the evening news. She asked a lot of questions, but was told in no uncertain terms to go away. Dad was livid, and flatly refused to watch the TV that evening.

On the third day, they gave up the hunt. As Dad said over breakfast, while rain spattered against the window, they were just wasting time. Until someone saw the creature again, there was no way of knowing where it might be. Mum nodded in agreement, then looked across the table and said, "Are you all right, Andy? You're very quiet."

"Am I?" Andy raised his head. "I'm fine, Mum. I was just – um – thinking."

In fact he wasn't all right, not entirely. For the last few days he'd been getting headaches. They weren't bad headaches, and they never lasted long, but they were happening too often for comfort. They were unpredictable, as well. A couple of times he'd felt the dull, throbbing pain in his temples at mealtimes, once it hit him while he was in the yard, and this morning he'd woken up at four o'clock with a feeling that someone was banging on the inside of his skull and trying to get out.

He knew he should have told someone about it. But Mum or Dad would have hauled him straight off to the doctor, and that would probably mean pills and tests and heaven alone knew what else. On balance, Andy decided, he'd rather put up with the headaches.

But they were a nuisance all the same. They made him tense and ratty, and unable to con-centrate properly. Now and then when they came, he felt sick, too. And occasionally he felt *scared* – a kind of fluttering, panicky sensation in the pit of his stomach that made him want to run away and hide somewhere until he calmed down. That didn't make any sense at all.

He had another headache this morning, and this one was lasting longer than they usually did. The sick feeling hadn't come, though; instead, he seemed to be unusually hungry, and all through the morning he kept raiding the fridge and the cupboards, nibbling whatever he thought Mum was least likely to notice. He didn't want sweet things, like biscuits. It was savoury food he craved – crisps or peanuts or cheese. But after a while he decided that they weren't quite right, either. He'd *love* a pork pie and a couple of sausage rolls, like the ones the local baker sold. In fact, he decided, he'd go into the village and get himself something really tasty.

He was putting on his waterproof when Fiz appeared.

"You going somewhere?" she asked.

"Just to the village," Andy told her.

"Oh, right. Can I come?"

He looked at her dubiously. "It's raining," he said.

"It's only water, isn't it? And I've got an anorak."

"I'm cycling, though."

"So who says I can't ride a bike? I know there's a couple of spare ones in the barn; I've seen them." Fiz grinned. "I might be a soft Southerner, but I'm not completely useless!"

Andy grinned back. A bit of company might put him in a better mood.

"Come on, then," he said. "Get your anorak, and I'll meet you outside."

They didn't talk much as they cycled towards the village. The road was too narrow and twisty to ride abreast safely, so Andy led the way while Fiz, on Martin's battered old bike, followed behind. She obviously wasn't used to hills; Andy could hear her puffing like a steam engine on the steep bits. But she'd have been hopping mad if he'd offered to slow down for her. He smiled to himself. He was actually getting to like Fiz. She was friendly, she joined in – she'd even given up her trendy gear and now wore jeans and sweatshirts and trainers, like anyone who lived in the country. All right, the specs still looked silly (he thought, anyway) but she said she was blind as a bat without them, so it couldn't be helped. On the whole, she was pretty OK.

The rain had slackened off by the time they reached Fossewell. Fiz headed for the post office, to get postcards for her parents and school friends, while Andy went into the baker's. They'd sold out of pork pies, so he bought four sausage rolls, and ate half of the first one before he even emerged from the shop.

For half an hour or so they walked round the village, Fiz looking at everything and stopping to peer in every shop window. But then the rain began to get heavier again, and this time it didn't look like relenting.

"Better get back," Andy said. "Unless you want to leave it a bit longer, then swim for it?"

They started back the way they'd come, heads down against the rain. Again, they didn't talk as they rode, but a couple of miles out of the village Andy heard Fiz calling to him.

"Andy! Stop a minute!"

They were on the crown of a hill; it had been a steep climb and Andy was only too glad to pull up. They lugged their bikes on to the verge and he said, "What's up? Puffed?"

"No." She was taking off her glasses. "But I need to wipe these; I can't see a thing!"

"Oh, right." He waited while she fished a tissue out of her pocket and rubbed the glasses dry.

"That's better." She put them on again, then looked over the hedge. "Wow, what a view! All that rolling country, going on for ever and ever!" She fumbled in her anorak. "Hang on while I take a picture."

"In this weather?" Andy said incredulously. "It'll just be a grey blob!"

She ignored him and pulled out a small but expensive-looking camera. Putting it to her eye, she panned it round. The shutter clicked, clicked again, then she turned to look at him.

"Is this anywhere near where your dad's sheep were killed?" she asked.

Andy looked at her in dismay. "How do you know about that?"

"Your mum told me the other day, after I put my foot in it with your dad," Fiz explained. "And don't worry – I won't say another word in front of him. But you don't mind talking about it, do you?"

Did he? Andy wasn't sure . . . and suddenly, for no apparent reason, his headache came back. "Well. . ." he said dubiously.

Fiz took that for an OK. "Something raided

your farm the other night, didn't it? Your mum told me that, too; she said it killed three chickens." Fiz paused. "And she said you saw it."

An unpleasant feeling clutched at Andy's stomach. "I didn't *see* it," he said evasively. "It was just. . ."

"What?" Fiz pressed. "Oh, go on, tell me!"

He didn't want to tell her. The headache was getting worse, he felt queasy, and he just wanted to jump back on his bike and ride away. But he couldn't.

"Look," he said, "there was something in the yard. But it was pitch dark and I didn't get a proper look. It could have been anything."

"But what do you think it is?"

Glowing, alien eyes. A menacing snarl. A flicker of a spotted coat. . . Abruptly the ache in Andy's skull flared to a pounding pain that made his eyes water. He gasped, clutching at his head, and Fiz's eyes widened.

"Andy? What's the matter?"

"Nnnh – nothing!" The pain was fading. But now he *had* to get away. It didn't matter what Fiz thought: he needed to *go*.

He swung round, meaning to grab his bike and ride off. But as his fingers closed on the

handlebars, Fiz hissed sharply, "Andy! Look –
what's that?"

Andy whipped round. She was pointing over
the fields. Something was moving in the
distance, in the shelter of one of the stone
walls. It slunk along, low to the ground. And it
looked as if it had a long tail. . .

"What is it?" Fiz breathed. "You don't
think. . ."

Pain hammered in Andy's head again – and
suddenly it was as if something else was there,
too. Another mind, locking with his. And an
image started to form in his head. . .

"It's nothing!" The words came out almost
before he knew what he was saying, and his
teeth started to chatter uncontrollably. "I-I-It's a
sheepdog. Just a sheepdog."

"That's not a dog! Look at its tail! And its
coat – it's got *spots*!" Fiz whirled to face him.
"Andy, it's the Fiend! It is, it *is*!"

"No!" Andy cried. "No, it isn't!"

But Fiz took no notice. Wildly excited, she
raced to the wall and climbed up, brandishing
her camera. "Oh, God, if I can get a photo –
it'll be the proof everyone's looking for!"

"*NO!*" Andy screamed. And before he
realized what he was doing, he flung himself

forward, scrambling on to the wall and snatching at Fiz's camera.

"Hey, what are you – *oww!*" She yelped as his hand clamped on her wrist and he tried to shake the camera out of her grasp.

"You mustn't, you mustn't – leave it alone!" Andy shouted. His vision had gone crazy; it was as though he was seeing Fiz through two sets of eyes at once. He was frightened, angry, desperate – he heard himself snarl at her, and they struggled, swaying perilously on the grassy wall top. Then suddenly Fiz pulled herself free, and Andy lost his balance. He fell; the ground spun to meet him and he landed on all fours.

And as he staggered upright, the panic hit him.

"Andy!" Fiz yelled. But Andy didn't hear. He was stumbling towards his bike, yanking it upright, climbing on. He didn't even look as he swung the bike on to the road. He didn't hear the approaching car engine.

Fiz screamed, "*Andy, look OUT!*"

7

The car was moving fast – much too fast for the road conditions. The driver saw Andy just in time. He swerved to avoid him – and swiped past the bike with centimetres to spare.

"Ohahh-WAAAH!" Andy wailed. The bike wobbled out of control and crashed back on to the verge, and the car flashed past. Three little kids pulled faces from the back window as it sped on down the hill.

And in the distance, a long, sleek shape left the shelter of the wall, streaking swiftly away and out of sight.

"Prat!" Fiz yelled furiously after the disappearing road-hog. She ran to where Andy was groggily sitting up. "Are you all right? Did it hit you?"

"N-No. . ." Andy had a bruise or two, but only from falling off the bike. "I'm OK." He paused, blinking. "What happened?"

"You acted like a total nutter, that's what happened!" Fiz told him indignantly. "Trying to snatch my camera – what the hell got into you?"

"Snatch your camera?" he echoed. "I didn't! Did I. . .?" He couldn't remember anything about it. The last thing he *could* remember was Fiz stopping to clean her glasses. After that, everything was a blank until the car had hurtled past.

Fiz knelt down on the grass and stared at him. "You must've got concussion," she said worriedly. "You can't ride your bike like this."

"I'm all right, honest," Andy insisted. "It was only the shock. . ." He swallowed. He *had* to find out what was going on. "Look," he said urgently, "just tell me what happened. What I did. It's important."

Fiz was still worried, but she told him the whole story. Andy listened with growing anxiety, and fragments of memory started to come back. He'd *had* to stop Fiz from taking any pictures. He didn't know why, but at that moment it had been the only thing in the world he'd cared about. And he'd been frightened. What was the matter with him?

Fiz said, "I think it's about time you levelled with me, Andy. There's something going on — and I want to know what it is!"

Andy was in an awful dilemma. He wanted to talk to someone about the weird things that had been happening to him. Keeping quiet was a strain, and Fiz was easy to talk to. But would she believe a word? She'd put the whole thing down to the bump on the head when he'd fallen out of bed that night. Either that, or she'd say he was out of his mind.

Which maybe he was. . .

Miserably, Andy admitted to himself that telling Fiz the whole story could be asking for trouble and he daren't do it. But he had to say something that would explain — or seem to — his weird behaviour a few minutes ago.

He thought fast, and an answer came to him.

"Look," he said, hoping desperately that she'd believe him, "I grabbed your camera because I . . . I got scared." That bit was true, at least. "I know we saw something, and I think it's the same thing that killed the sheep and the chickens. But if the papers and the TV found out . . . well, they'd go crazy. They'd be swarming all over the place in three seconds flat. You know what my dad thinks about that. So just imagine what he'd do if it was your photo that started it all!"

Fiz frowned, considering. "You mean, you were thinking about me?"

"Well . . . sort of. I mean, I'd get it in the neck, too, because Dad'd blame me for bringing you up here in the first place."

"Ah. Right. I get the picture." She grinned suddenly. "Picture – geddit?" Andy didn't laugh, and after a second or two she shrugged. "OK. So what you're saying is, you don't trust me not to blab to the media."

Andy turned red. "Well. . . I can't be sure, can I? And when you get people nosing around, like that godawful Kristie Kerr. . ."

"Who?" Fiz looked blank.

"The TV news reporter that Dad ran into yesterday."

"Oh, right. Well, fair enough. I suppose there's no reason why you should trust me. But I wasn't going to go yelling it from the rooftops or anything. I just wanted to get a picture. Anyone would."

"Sorry," said Andy.

"It doesn't matter." Her face brightened. "Anyway, I fired off a couple of shots before you grabbed me."

Andy tensed. "You did?"

"Yeah. So maybe there'll be something to look at after all. Be interesting to see, won't it?" Fiz got to her feet. "Come on; let's get going. I don't know about you, but I'm getting soaked sitting here!"

She started towards her bike. Andy said in dismay, "Fiz. . ."

"Yeah?" She looked at him. Brightly. Innocently. He could trust her. Surely he could. . .?

"Nothing," he said. "Let's go."

Andy opened his eyes, looked at his bedside clock, and thought: *Oh, no, not again!*

Two a.m. This waking up in the middle of the night business was getting to be a habit. And there was no reason this time. No nightmares, no noises in the yard. Everything was quiet.

Annoyed, he turned over and tried to go back to sleep. But he couldn't. His head was aching – not badly, but enough to irritate him.

And something else was nagging away at the back of his mind. A niggling worry that wouldn't let him alone.

If Fiz *had* got pictures of the animal, what was she going to do with them? She'd promised him that she wouldn't go babbling to the press and TV, but would she keep her promise? The chance to grab the limelight and become the "Finder of the Fossewell Fiend", or whatever, would be so tempting.

And Andy did not, not, *not* want it to happen.

Suddenly the headache increased to a dull insistent throb, and a sharp mental picture snapped into his mind. He saw himself, climbing – no, *leaping* – on to the wall, lunging at Fiz, trying to grab the camera. He remembered the swaying struggle, Fiz shouting at him, him snarling at her. Then losing his balance, falling, landing on hands and feet, and – and –

The picture zipped away and Andy found himself sitting upright, blinking and gasping as if he'd just surfaced from under dark, cold water. There was a new thought in his head, so strong that it overwhelmed everything else. *He had to stop Fiz from getting that film developed!* It didn't matter how; it didn't even matter why. It just had to be done.

He looked around. Strangely, he could see his bedroom quite clearly without a lamp. Everyone else would be fast asleep.

And Fiz's camera was downstairs on the kitchen dresser. . .

The landing was darker than Andy's bedroom, but it didn't seem to matter; he could still see clearly. For a moment it occurred to him that that was *very* odd, but he had more important things to concentrate on.

He tiptoed along the landing and down the stairs. He was unusually aware of every tiny sound. Wind in the eaves. Roof tiles creaking. Windows rattling slightly in their frames. He'd heard Martin snoring as he passed his door, and it had sounded as loud as a chainsaw. Weird . . . but probably it was just nerves, heightening everything the way they often did.

As Andy eased the kitchen door open, a dark shape leaped to its feet. Since the chicken raid, Dad had put the two adult sheepdogs, Cap and Bran, in the barn at nights, in case the intruder came back. But Meg, the half-grown pup, still slept in the kitchen. Andy could see her staring at him, and for a moment he felt almost . . . scared of her. Then, to his astonishment, Meg bared her teeth in a threatening snarl.

"Hey!" Andy hissed. "Hey, Meg, it's only me! Quiet, girl!"

Meg hesitated. A low growl rumbled in her throat.

"Meg!" Andy said again. His heart was thumping. This was crazy!

Very slowly and carefully he put out a hand to the collie. For an awful moment he thought she'd lunge at him – but suddenly she seemed to realize who he was. The snarl vanished, her tail wagged tentatively; then she came wriggling to greet him. Andy sighed thankfully.

"That's better!" Daft animal; she must have thought he was a burglar! He rubbed her ears, then turned to the dresser.

The camera was there. Picking it up, he looked for the catch that would open the film compartment. Meg was still staring at him. She made him feel uneasy for some reason, and he seemed to be all thumbs as he found the catch and fumbled with it.

"Come on, come *on*! Stupid thing. . ." *Ah!* Got it. The camera flipped open and he pulled the film out. He didn't care what Fiz would say, or whether she'd guess who had sabotaged her pictures. All that mattered was to make sure they were thoroughly ruined.

Andy started to pull the roll of film out of the canister, watching as it uncoiled in a long, dark snake. It was about half-way out when he began to feel dizzy. The floor swam, the walls swelled and receded – and a feeling like panic rose chokingly inside him.

Andy gasped and swayed on his feet. His hands clenched uncontrollably – and suddenly he wasn't tugging gently at the film, but *clawing* it, tearing it, ripping it from the canister and shredding it to pieces.

"No, no, no!" He was repeating the word over and over again, almost shouting, unable to stop the wild fury that had taken him over. *Claw* it, *destroy* it; get it out and *trample* it – he hated it, he was frightened of it, because it would give him away to *them*. . .

Meg snarled again, and the sound shattered the frenzy in Andy's head. The collie was confronting him, hackles up. Andy stumbled back and collided with the dresser, rattling all the cups. Meg took a step towards him.

"Meg, it's me, it's Andy! Meg, stop it!"

The snarl became a growl, and the growl turned into a ferocious bark.

And from upstairs came the sound of running feet.

Terror punched through Andy. He didn't stop to think; he *couldn't* think – there was no reason in him. The camera dropped from his hand and he launched himself away from the dresser, jumping over Meg and racing to the back door. He was through the door in less than a second, and as the collie sprang after him he slammed it in her face.

Rain whirled around him, and the yard was cold and dark, but Andy didn't care. All he knew was that *they* were coming after him, and *they* mustn't catch him. Nothing else counted. Nothing else in his whole crazy, distorted, terrifying world.

A volley of hysterical barking echoed behind the house door, and from the barn the other two dogs joined in. A hammering pain pounded through Andy's head.

Then he turned and raced away into the night.

8

"It was definitely over here somewhere. The dogs had the scent."

"But they've lost it now, Dad. Look at them – just going round in circles. The rain's washed it out."

Dad muttered something, and Andy shut his eyes, holding his breath and struggling not to make the smallest sound. He heard boots approaching the wall, and he hunched down lower, trying to make himself as small as possible. *Don't look over; oh, please, don't look over. . .*

"It's no good, Dad." Martin's voice was horribly close, and when Andy dared to peek up, he saw the shaft of a torch beam swinging over the wall top above him. "It'll be miles away by now. Let's give up."

There was a pause. Andy prayed desperately that the noise of his heart thumping wouldn't give him away. Then Dad sighed, and he heard a click . . . the safety catch of a shotgun being put on. A wave of cold sweat washed over him.

"All right," said Dad. "Better check everything's OK in the yard, though I don't think it's done any harm this time. Lucky the dogs heard it early. Come on, Bran! Heel, Cap!"

Their voices and footsteps faded into the night as they went away, and Andy let his breath go in a dizzy rush. This was completely, unspeakably, impossibly *insane*! To be out here in the middle of the night, crouching behind a wall, soaked and freezing. And terrified half out of his wits, because he'd believed – he'd *really* believed – that his dad and his brother were enemies who were out to kill him! What sort of madness was this?

He started to stand up, but suddenly felt so sick and giddy that he had to grab at the top of the stone wall to steady himself. He thought he was going to throw up, but he didn't, and after a minute the awful feeling faded, leaving him drained and weak. Better get back to the house, and fast. If anyone missed him, he'd never be able to explain.

He started to feel his way towards the gate. No question of going straight over the wall the way he'd done a few minutes ago; he didn't have the strength any more. He couldn't see in the dark now, either. Have to grope along until he found the gate.

His hand had just closed on the gate's top bar when something made him stop. A faint noise, like an exhaled breath. . . Andy's skin prickled, and slowly he turned round.

There was nothing behind him. But he could sense a presence, and it wasn't far away. Something was watching. And Andy had encountered it before. . .

The dark scene in front of him slipped sideways, and suddenly it was as if he were several metres away, looking back at himself. He saw a hunched, cowering little figure, and he didn't like it. Didn't trust it. It was one of *them*, and it was his enemy.

LEAVE ME ALONE!

The desperate, angry thought rose in his head, but *he* wasn't thinking it. Something else was – another mind that was mixing and

72

muddling itself with his own. He seemed to be split in two. One half was Andy, who stood trembling in front of the gate with his jaw hanging open – and the other was a creature, fierce, but at the same time every bit as scared as he was. He felt what it was feeling. Confusion. Suspicion. Hostility.

And *hunger*.

"N-no. . ." Andy stammered. His fingers scrabbled for the gate latch. "No, don't hurt me! Please don't!" Suddenly the latch flipped up and he almost fell over as the gate swung open at his back. He staggered, regained his balance. . .

And realized that the presence was no longer there. The creature had melted into the night, and vanished.

Andy stared at the place where he thought it had been, but there was nothing to see except darkness. He swallowed hard. Then he turned and raced towards the house.

The family, and Fiz, were in the kitchen, and as Andy rushed in at the back door, he ran slap into Mum.

"Andy!" she said as he rebounded. "Where on earth have you been?"

Someone must have looked in his room.

Andy shut his eyes, praying he could get out of this hole. "I – er – went out after Dad and Martin," he fluffed. "When the – when—"

Mum interrupted. "You just went after them? Look at your feet! And your T-shirt; it's filthy! Honestly, Andy, how stupid can you get?"

"Oh, leave him alone, Mum," said Martin. "No one else stopped to get dressed, did they?"

"At least you and Dad put wellies on!" Mum persisted.

"And I've told you before, Andrew, about running out in the dark when it might be dangerous," Dad added sternly. He had unloaded the shotgun and was locking it away. "I could have mistaken you for that animal!"

You don't know how nearly right you are! Andy thought with a shudder. He hung his head. "Sorry."

Mum relented. "Well, no harm done, I suppose," she said. "You'd better go back to bed. You too, Fiz; you must have had quite a fright when – oh." She stopped, looking at what Fiz was holding. "Oh, dear – what's happened to your camera?"

"I don't know," said Fiz. She had the mangled remains of the film in one hand and

74

the camera, with its back still hanging open, in the other. She was looking very steadily at Andy.

"Meg must have knocked it down when she got excited," said Mum. "What a shame! I *am* sorry, Fiz."

"It doesn't matter, Auntie Jo." Fiz's gaze didn't shift from Andy, and she added through clenched teeth, "There was nothing important on it."

Andy knew he'd turned as red as a beetroot. He mumbled something that sounded vaguely like "'Night", and bolted upstairs. But Fiz followed, and caught him up before he could reach his bedroom. Fists on hips, face like thunder, she squared up to him.

"Andy. I want a word with you. *Now,*" she insisted.

Andy squirmed – and another voice came to his rescue.

"All right, you two?" Martin had come up the stairs behind them. "Good. Oh, Fiz – Mum says to tell you that she's got a spare camera film in the cupboard downstairs, and you're welcome to have it."

"That's nice of her." Fiz smiled. "But it's all right, honestly; I've got some more."

"OK." Martin grinned. "But it's there if you want it. 'Night, then."

" 'Night. Thanks," said Fiz.

She watched as Martin went into his room, then swung round to have another go at Andy.

But Andy had gone. And his bedroom door was firmly shut and bolted.

Andy thought he was dreaming. He was out in the fields, and again the world looked all wrong, as if he were seeing it through someone else's eyes. This time, though, he knew he wasn't a sheep. He could see them in the distance, but he wasn't one of them. He was something else.

He was lying down in the shelter of a stone wall, with his face close to the ground. His heart beat quickly as he watched the sheep, and there was saliva in his mouth and a gnawing in his stomach. He was hungry. *Very* hungry. It had been days since he'd had enough food to make the gnawing go away; those two little squawking, feathery things hadn't been much more than a mouthful, and *they* had frightened him off before he could eat any more. He was very wary of *them*. He didn't want to look for his next meal in a place

76

where *they* might find him. But he had to eat soon. He just had to.

He looked up at the sky and saw that the moon was setting. Good. That would give him more cover. It would be dawn soon, but he still had enough time. The Andy part of his mind tried to ask how he could see so well in darkness, but the part that wasn't Andy ignored the question. He was moving now, slowly but steadily, following the line of the wall and being careful to keep hidden. He could smell the sheep, and the thought of so much lovely meat made his mouth water. They didn't know he was here. Stupid things – they'd already forgotten about him. This time, he thought, he'd get himself a bigger one. . .

Somewhere outside the mind of the stalking predator, the real Andy watched what was happening with a mixture of fascination and horror. It was a hideous feeling; he was the animal, and yet he wasn't, and the two sensations were becoming more tangled every moment. The human part of him wanted to scream, *Stop it, stop it, I don't want this to happen!* But another part, slinking and hunting and seeing in the dark, was going to attack the sheep. And there was nothing anyone could do to stop it.

Closer and closer he crept, until the nearest sheep were only a few metres away. Crouch . . . tense. . . One of the sheep raised its head. It stared into the darkness uncertainly. It started to get to its feet. . .

LEAP! It was like launching himself from a springboard; he was flying through the air, muscles powering, excitement exploding through him as he hurled himself at his prey. The sheep tried to turn and run, but it was too late. He landed with a huge impact, heard a terrified bleat. Then his powerful jaws opened. He lunged! He *BIT*—

He woke up.

For several minutes Andy lay shivering with shock. He didn't want to think about what had happened, but he couldn't shake off the memory of it. And an awful realization was dawning on him. Because he was absolutely and appallingly convinced that it hadn't been a dream. It had actually been happening!

Andy stumbled out of bed and flung the window open to let in some fresh air. The sky was getting light and there were noises of someone around in the yard. Dad, probably. He'd be going up to the fields soon, to check on the sheep. Andy knew what he would find. The animal was out there now, this very minute, eating the prey it had killed. Andy knew, because he'd *been* there.

He emerged from the bathroom. On the landing, Fiz was waiting for him.

"I heard you get up." She had her arms folded, and glared at him as if he was Public Enemy Number 1. "You sneaked away last night. But you're not going anywhere now. Not until I've had an explanation."

Andy leaned against the wall. He was feeling dizzy. "I can't," he mumbled. "Honest, Fiz, I – right now, I just *can't*."

"Bilge!" said Fiz. "I'm not falling for that trick. Now look, Andy Thorpe—"

"It *isn't* a trick!" said Andy desperately.

Maybe his voice or his face told Fiz something then, because she frowned and said, "Hey – you all right? You look awful!"

"I *feel* awful!" Oh God, what was he going to do? He couldn't keep this to himself any longer. He needed help. He needed someone to tell him that the insane theory in his head couldn't be true!

Andy made a decision. "Look," he said, trying to get his voice under control, "there *is* something going on, but it – it's going to be very, very hard to explain."

"I'm listening," said Fiz.

"I know. But I can't tell you about it now, when someone might come along and hear us."

She raised her eyebrows. "That serious, huh?"

He nodded. "After breakfast, come out with me. On the bikes. We'll go somewhere quiet, and I'll tell you then." *If I can*, he added to himself.

"Well. . ." She wavered, then gave in. "OK. But if you run out on me again—"

"I won't, I promise." Andy started towards his bedroom, then paused. "Oh, one thing. We'd better keep out of Dad's way when he comes back from the fields this morning."

"Yeah? Why?"

"Because. . ." He swallowed. "Because he's going to find something there that he won't like one bit."

9

Andy was a bag of nerves as he waited for Dad to come back from the fields. By the time breakfast was ready there was still no sign of him, and Mum was getting concerned.

"I hope nothing's wrong," she said as she dished up scrambled eggs and toast.

Andy and Fiz looked at each other over the table, but neither spoke. Martin forked up a mouthful of egg and said through it, "He's probably forgotten the time; you know what Dad's like. Mmm! This is good. Come on, Andy, you're not eating!"

"I'm – er – not very hungry," Andy muttered.

"Oh well, if you don't want yours, I'll have

it!" Cheerfully Martin scooped Andy's helping on to his own plate. "Nothing like a good breakfast!"

Andy thought of the sheep, and wished he hadn't. But Mum was looking curiously at him, so he buttered a piece of toast and managed to force it down, to put her off the scent. He had just started on a cup of tea that he didn't want, but which had been poured out for him, when he jumped violently. Something had *zing*ed past his head with a high-pitched whine, and at the same moment he felt a jolt in his shoulder, like brushing against a stinging nettle.

Mum looked at him in surprise. "What's up with you?"

"I don't know – I thought something just buzzed me." Inexplicably, Andy's hands were shaking. He hid them under the table. "Made me jump."

"A wasp?" said Martin.

"Don't be silly, Martin; there aren't any wasps around at this time of year." Mum poured herself more tea. "I expect Andy imagined it."

Andy didn't say anything more, but he knew it hadn't been imagination. Something had happened just now. And there was a connection with the creature. He just knew there was.

The roar of a diesel engine sounded outside, and Mum glanced out of the window.

"Ah, there's Dad," she said. "He's in a hurry!" Her expression changed. "Something *has* happened. . ."

Andy's heart sank as Dad jumped out of the Land Rover and came running to the house. He'd found exactly what Andy had known he'd find. Another dead sheep.

Only this time there was a difference.

"The animal was *there*!" Dad told them breathlessly. "Right next to the sheep it had killed! It ran when it saw me, of course – but I got a shot at it."

Andy gripped the edge of the table, and Martin asked eagerly, "Did you hit it?"

Dad shook his head. "I don't think so. But it was close; I can't have missed by much. And I saw where it went. That woody valley, where the stream gets wider – it's no more than five minutes since I saw it, so there's a good chance it's still somewhere around there. Get the other gun, Martin. We're going after it!"

Andy felt all the colour draining from his face. He wanted to protest, to shout, "No,

Dad, don't!" but his throat was frozen and he couldn't get the words out. *No more than five minutes*, Dad had said. And at almost the same moment, something had whizzed past Andy's ear.

Something very much like a shot. . .

As Martin ran to fetch the other shotgun, Mum said, "Do you think it was the same animal that raided the chickens?"

Dad nodded. "I'd take any bet on it. And I'll tell you something else." He swung round to look at Andy. "You were right the other night. It isn't a dog!"

"What is it, then?" Mum asked anxiously. "Not – not a wolf?"

"No. It's spotted, like Andy said. And it's got a long, thin tail."

"A leopard?"

"Maybe. Or something even bigger."

"Phil," Mum said uneasily, "don't you think we ought to tell the police? A rogue dog's one thing, but *this*—"

"No!" Dad snapped. "You know what would happen then – we'd get tied up in red tape, and nothing would be done! No, Jo – no police, no reporters, nobody! We'll deal with it."

Fiz looked dismayed. "But Uncle Phil, they might be able to catch it alive," she said.

Dad stared at her. "Catch it alive?"

"Yes. If it *is* a leopard, then killing it seems – well, they're so rare, aren't they?"

The stare became a glower. "Rare?" Dad echoed. "That animal is killing my sheep! The only thing it's going to be is *dead*!" He swung round as Martin came hurrying back. "Ready? Right – let's get going!"

As the Land Rover screeched away, Andy found he was shaking again, and this time he couldn't stop. He was frightened. Not just the way Mum was – in case Dad and Martin got hurt. He was frightened for himself. Because now, he was sure he knew what was happening to him.

And he knew his life was in danger.

Andy and Fiz left the house a few minutes later, and walked along a footpath that ran from the farmyard towards the Ridge. They didn't talk until they came to a gate between two fields, then Fiz stopped abruptly.

"Andy," she said, "your dad . . . he *can't* kill that poor animal! Not if it's so rare and special. It isn't *fair*!"

Andy leaned on the gate, staring at the pastures and a grey-green smudge of trees in the distance. He agreed with Fiz – and for more reasons than she knew.

He'd planned to tell her everything because he wanted her to convince him that his theory was impossible. Now, though, the situation had changed. Now, he didn't think it *was* impossible. He believed it, and nothing anyone could say would make him change his mind. But what could Fiz actually do? To start with, she wouldn't believe his story. No one in their right senses would. It was just too crazy.

"Andy?" Fiz said. "Did you hear what I said?"

"Yeah," Andy replied flatly.

"Then what are we going to do about it?"

She'd forgotten yesterday's incident and the explanation she wanted, but that all tied in. And Andy had to start somewhere. . .

"Look," he said, "I told you last night that I've got something to say and it's going to be difficult. It's about the animal. And me. And your camera."

"What?" She frowned, baffled.

He turned to face her. "I agree with you about not wanting it to be killed. I'm *terrified*

86

of it being killed, because. . ." He faltered, swallowed. "Fiz, if I tell you the whole lot, will you promise to listen, and not laugh at me? At least till I've finished."

Her expression was deadly serious – and full of curiosity. "Yes," she said.

"All right. Here goes, then. It all started when I had this awful dream. . ."

She didn't interrupt him once as, stumblingly, he got the story out. Andy knew he wasn't telling it very well; and the more he said, the crazier the whole thing sounded, even to him. But he ploughed on, and finally came to the last and most important part of the tale.

"I think," he said, "that somehow I've become . . . linked with the creature. I can see what it sees, and feel what it feels. And I'm scared, Fiz. I'm scared because . . . I think that whatever happens to it, might . . . happen to me, as well."

Silence fell. Fiz didn't say a word, and Andy thought unhappily: *That's it. She'll tell me I'm barking mad. She's got to.*

Fiz was staring over the gate now, but she wasn't looking at the scenery. At last, just when he thought he couldn't stand the tension any longer, she spoke.

"You've got to admit it takes a bit of swallowing."

Andy sighed. "Yeah. I know. And I don't expect you believe a word of it."

"I didn't say that, did I?" She swung round. "Truth is, Andy, I don't know what I believe. But I'll tell you one thing. I don't think you're making any of it up. I mean, why would you? If you wanted an excuse for what you did to my camera, you'd have come up with something I'd fall for, not some horror-movie plot like this!"

"So. . ." said Andy cautiously.

"So *you* obviously think it's really happening. And that's got to mean one of two things. One — that bang on the head's affected your brain. Or two — it really is true, and somehow you've got your mind tangled up with the mind of the Fossewell Fiend." She pursed her lips and whistled. "What a story that'd make for the media!"

"Fiz!" Andy said in horror. "You can't—"

"Of course I won't, stupid! What d'you take me for? Anyway," she added, "they'd just tell us to go away and stop winding them up."

He let his breath out. "Yeah. Yeah, they would."

"The weirdest part of it's what happened

this morning," Fiz continued thoughtfully. "You sensing what you did at the same time that the animal must have been attacking the sheep. That's *creepy*."

"And thinking that something zinged past me," Andy added.

"Almost exactly when your dad fired that shot. . . Mmm," Fiz mused. "Have you had any other weird feelings since then?"

He shook his head. "No. It only seems to happen when it – the creature – gets excited, or frightened. Or –" he suppressed a shiver – "when I'm close to it."

"Which you've been a few times." She looked over the gate again. "Where do you think it is now?"

"I've no idea. Probably lying up in the woods, like Dad said."

"That's where your dad and Martin are going looking for it, right?"

"Right."

"So what happens if they find it? If it gets – what did you say? Excited, or frightened?"

Andy's flesh crawled. "I . . . don't know," he whispered. He licked his lips, which felt horribly dry. "You're talking as if you *do* believe it."

"No-o. But. . ."

"What?" he prompted.

"Well. . ." She tapped her fingers on the gate, looking uneasy. "We can't afford to tell ourselves that it isn't true, can we? We can't take the chance. Or rather, you can't. Because if your dad killed it. . ."

Andy drew a deep breath and made himself say it. "I might die, too."

There was a very long silence after that, as they leaned on the gate, keeping their thoughts to themselves. At last, Fiz spoke.

"We've got to find a way to stop your dad from shooting it," she said sombrely.

"Tell me about it!" Andy agreed with feeling. "But the problem is, how? You heard him this morning, when you said your bit about catching it alive." He laughed harshly. "A few days ago I'd have agreed with him."

"Would you?" Fiz looked shocked.

"Well, yeah. Because it had killed our sheep."

"But it's got to eat to stay alive! Hunting's natural to it, and sheep must be a pretty easy target. It isn't fair to hunt it down and shoot it, just for trying to survive!"

She was right, but the memory of his last

vision came back sharply to Andy. The stalk, the leap, the kill – he shivered. "OK," he said, pushing the clammy feeling away. "I agree with you – I would, even if this wasn't happening to me. But no one's ever going to convince Dad. If we tried, he wouldn't even listen."

"Then we'll have to talk to someone who will," said Fiz firmly.

"No! I won't let you go to the press or TV—"

"I don't mean them. I mean someone who knows about wild animals. Someone who could catch it alive."

Andy considered that idea. "The RSPCA, or wildlife experts, or something?"

"Exactly." Fiz rested her chin on her arms, thinking hard. "The problem is, how to do it without the police getting involved. I know what your dad said about red tape and nothing being done, but I think they'd get marksmen, or whatever, out here straight away – you know, public safety and all that. So we've got to find a way to—"

She didn't get any further, because at that moment a distant shot echoed out across the fields. From here it wasn't a loud noise, but it was enough to make Fiz jump like a startled rabbit.

"*Oh!* What was that? They're not—" She had swung round. "Andy?" Her eyes widened in alarm. "*Andy!*"

Andy wasn't looking at her any more. He was lying flat on the ground, face down, arms flung out and legs sprawled.

And he wasn't moving.

10

"Stop! *Stop!*"

With no thought for her own safety, Fiz ran out into the road as the sound of the car engine approached round the bend. All she cared about was that Andy was lying unconscious a hundred metres away, and she had to get help!

The car appeared, and there was a squeal of brakes as it skidded to a halt. It was a yellow sports car, and the driver was a young woman with blonde hair. Andy would have recognized her immediately. Fiz, however, did not.

She raced up to the car and gasped breathlessly, "Oh, please, can you help me? It's my cousin – he's had an accident!"

* * *

Andy was only half conscious. He kept hearing snatches of talk, but they faded away every few seconds, so he couldn't follow clearly. Two people, he thought, saying things like: "Careful! Can you lift his legs?" or "That's it; now fix the seat-belt. . ."

He tried to remember what had happened to him. He'd been talking to Fiz, then there had been the far-off sound of a shot, and he'd just . . . blacked out. He hadn't *been* shot, he knew that much. Nothing hurt. He'd simply keeled over for no apparent reason, and now he felt muddled and weak, as if he'd been rescued from drowning or something.

There was a bit more talk that he didn't catch, then came a steady noise, a joggling sensation and the feeling of wind in his face. He was in a car, he thought. Being taken somewhere. That was all right, then. And it would be so easy to go back to sleep. . .

"So what exactly happened?" Kristie Kerr asked Fiz as they drove, slowly because of Andy, towards the farm.

"He – um – fell off the gate," said Fiz miserably. "And he hit his head on a stone."

"Ah. So what were you two doing up that way?"

"Just walking."

"Mmm. I saw some men with guns over there a while ago, and they were out the other day, too. Any idea what they were doing?"

Fiz squirmed uncomfortably in her seat. "Looking for rabbits, I expect."

"Rabbits. Right. Not anything else? Like . . . a big wild animal, for instance?" She smiled. "You see, Fiz, I'm a reporter. I work for Dales TV – my name's Kristie Kerr. And if there's anything interesting happening, it's my job to find out about it."

Fiz froze, staring at her with a horrified expression that told the reporter all she needed to know.

"Sorry," she said, quite kindly. "Your face is a dead giveaway! Something's going on, isn't it? Something you don't want to tell me?"

Fiz shut her eyes. "I *can't* tell you," she said. "I promised. . ."

"Promised who?"

"Andy." She shut her eyes. "And his dad – my Uncle Phil. If he knew I was even talking to you, he'd go crazy!"

"Well, seeing that I've rescued his son, I think that's a bit mean!" Kristie smiled again to show she was joking, or sort of. Then her face became sympathetic. "But it's bothering you, isn't it? The thing you're scared to tell me – you're worried about it."

She waited. For a few moments Fiz didn't speak. Then suddenly, in a rush, she blurted, "The farmers want to shoot it! I don't want that to happen!"

"*Shoot* it?" Kristie looked shocked. "But that's awful!"

"I know! But we can't make Uncle Phil see. . ." Fiz stopped in mid-sentence and gulped. "I shouldn't be telling you this."

"Oh, but you should!" said Kristie. "You see, I love animals, too, and I think it'd be terrible if the farmers just shot this poor creature!" She reached out with one hand and patted Fiz's shoulder sympathetically. "Look, Fiz – why don't you tell me a bit more about it? And maybe together we can come up with a way to help. . ."

Andy came to again in time to feel the car lurching over the farm track. The movement stopped with a jolt, and the dogs began to bark. Then footsteps came running, and through the confusion in his head he heard Mum shouting, "What's happened? What's *happened*?" Things got very mixed up for a while after that, and he'd been carried to the big sofa in the sitting room and made comfortable with umpteen blankets and cushions before he was able to work out what *had* happened.

Or rather, what Fiz was pretending had happened.

"We were climbing over the gate, Auntie Jo," he heard her say. "Andy slipped, I think. He fell off, and there were a lot of stones on the ground. He must have hit his head, so I ran to the nearest road and—"

"Luckily, I came along." It was the second voice he'd heard earlier. And with a shock, Andy recognized it.

"Well, Ms Kerr, I'm very grateful to you," Mum said awkwardly. "Oh, poor Andy! I hope he's going to be all right!"

"I don't think it's anything serious," Kristie Kerr reassured her. "I've had some first aid training, and I took a look at him. I didn't find any injury, except a bruise on his head, but it looks as if he did that a while ago."

No, Andy thought. *You wouldn't have found anything. Because there's nothing to find. . .*

Mum came to peer at him, but he pretended not to be aware of her. He'd heard her phoning the doctor, who was coming straight over, and that would be bad enough without Mum fussing around him as well.

"He's asleep," Mum said, dropping her voice to a whisper. "Probably the best thing. Well, Ms Kerr, we mustn't hold you up any more. I expect you're very busy. . ."

Kristie Kerr took the broad hint. "Yes, of course," she said brightly. "Glad to have helped, Mrs Thorpe. Bye, now."

Andy heard her and Mum leave the room, and opened one eye cautiously. Fiz was standing by the window, looking out and frowning.

"Fiz!" he whispered.

She whirled round and hurried towards him. "You're awake! Are you OK?"

"Yeah, I think so. Just a bit woozy, that's all. Hey, thanks for making up that story about the gate. Quick thinking." He pulled a face. "But Fiz – the woman who brought us back. You know who she is, don't you?"

Fiz nodded. "She told me."

"What a lousy piece of luck!" Suddenly agitated, he sat up. "You didn't give anything away, did you?"

"No!" Fiz said it a little bit too quickly and emphatically, but Mum came back at that moment, so Andy didn't see her face turn red.

"Andy!" Mum said. "Lie down *at once*! I don't want you to *move* till the doctor's seen you!"

Andy tried to protest that he was perfectly all right, but Mum wouldn't listen. She'd tie him down with the clothes-line if she had to, she said, but he was staying *put*. After a bit of arguing, Andy gave up. Fiz had gone up to her room, and anyway, he couldn't talk to her with Mum hovering. He just hoped that the doctor, when he came, wouldn't find anything wrong with him. Because he and Fiz had things to do. And they couldn't afford to waste any time.

Dr Roberts had been the village doctor for about eight million years. He was very cheerful, very old-fashioned, and was always joking that most things could be cured with a dose of Milk of Magnesia or a brisk, healthy walk. He checked Andy thoroughly, then straightened up.

"Nothing wrong with him at all!" he boomed bracingly at Mum. "He's even healthier than me! Well, no boy of his age ever died of falling off a gate, did they? Yes, yes, Andrew; of course you can get up. Go and climb another gate, I would – you obviously need some practice!"

Andy gave silent thanks, and as soon as Dr Roberts's car had driven off, he went upstairs to find Fiz.

"Andy?" she called out when she heard him approach, and her door opened. "Come on in. Are you all right? What did the doctor say?"

"He said I'm fine. Nothing wrong at all."

Fiz breathed out. "What a relief!"

"Too right! Look, Fiz, I've got to make sure – you *didn't* give anything away to that Kerr woman, did you?"

"I told you I didn't! Though—" she paused, and he said suspiciously, "'Though' what? Fiz, you haven't—"

"*No!*" she insisted. "But Andy, don't you think that maybe she's the sort of person we *ought* to talk to? I mean, she's with the TV, so she must have lots of contacts. If we told her about the animal, she might know people from the wildlife organizations—"

"Don't be crazy!" Andy interrupted. "She'd turn it into a story, and it'd be all over the news in five minutes!"

"She might not. If we asked."

Andy raised his eyes heavenwards, wondering how anyone could be so gullible. "Fiz, she's a reporter! No; we've got to do it by ourselves. We can't trust anyone else – and Kristie Kerr least of all."

Fiz looked thoroughly unhappy, but as she opened her mouth to argue again, they both heard the Land Rover turning into the yard. It stopped, and from the window Andy saw Dad and Martin getting out. He breathed a sigh of relief. If the hunt was over for the day, the animal – and he – were safe till tomorrow.

Dad looked up, saw him, and waved. "Andy! Come downstairs, quickly!"

What on earth. . .? "Come on," Andy said to Fiz. "Sounds like *something*'s happened."

It had. Dad and Martin were in the kitchen, already talking to Mum, when Andy and Fiz piled downstairs.

"What is it?" Andy asked.

Martin was excited and breathless. "We've seen the animal!" he said. "Close up – we were only a few metres from it!"

"*What?*" Andy's jaw dropped.

"And it isn't a leopard!" said Dad. "It's much bigger. It's a cat, all right, and it's got a spotted coat. But it's the size of a tiger!"

11

Dad and Martin had been combing the wooded valley again. Once they thought they saw the animal, and Martin had fired his gun. That, Andy realized, was the shot that had affected him. . . But there was nothing there. If the creature *had* been lurking, it had vanished back into the trees.

They'd kept hunting for another two hours. Then, when they were just about to give up, they really *had* seen it. They'd been scrambling down the stream bank, trying not to make too much noise, when there was a rustle in the undergrowth on the far side. They'd looked up – and there it was, crouched at the top of the opposite bank. Long, and sleek, with a gold-and-black spotted coat, staring at them with cold, gleaming eyes. Its ears were flattened against its skull, and as they stared in amazement it had opened its mouth and snarled softly. And it must have been at least three metres long.

"We're going to need help," Dad told Mum. "Four or five more men at least. I'll phone round the other farmers – get them over here to start planning."

Fiz's eyes widened in alarm and she started to say, "Uncle Phil—" But Andy's foot came down hard on her toe, and the protest turned into a yelp. Everyone else was too preoccupied to notice, and as soon as he could Andy took Fiz to one side and hissed, "Don't say anything! We've got to keep quiet!"

"But we're running out of time!"

Andy shook his head. "They won't do anything else today except talk. As soon as we can, we'll ring someone who can help us. There's a conservation trust not very far from here – they'll be best, I reckon. But *don't* let on to Dad!"

"All right." Fiz swallowed. "Sorry. I just got scared. . ."

"Well, you can't be half as scared as I am!"

Andy could hear Dad's voice on the phone, talking fast and urgently. The other farmers wouldn't take long to get over, then they'd all shut themselves in the sitting room and that would give Andy the chance to make his call.

Come on, he urged silently in his mind. *Hurry up and get here. And then I'll only need five minutes!*

". . . office hours are nine to four-thirty, Mondays to Fridays. If you would like to leave a message, please speak after the tone, and one of our staff will get back to you as soon as possible. Thank you for calling the—"

Andy slammed the receiver down before the recording finished, and turned to look helplessly at Fiz. "They've shut for the day," he said.

"Oh, no! Now what do we do?"

Andy shrugged. "Wait till tomorrow, I suppose. There's no point leaving a message if there's no one to hear it, and it'd take too long to explain." He glanced towards the closed sitting room door. "Wonder what they're deciding in there?"

"I don't think I want to know." Fiz shivered.

"Shall we go upstairs? At least we can talk privately there."

They mooched up to Andy's room. But when they tried to talk, neither of them could find anything to say. The trouble was, they both felt so helpless. The tension in them was building up to a suffocating pitch, but until tomorrow morning there was nothing they could do that was of any use.

Then, after about an hour, they heard the sound of men's voices downstairs.

"They've finished!" Andy jumped to his feet. "Come on – let's go and find out what's happened."

He didn't wait for Fiz but ran along the landing. Part of him was dreading what he might hear, but at the same time any news, however alarming, was better than being kept in the dark. The men were out in the yard, getting into their various vehicles. One of them, a farmer called Alf Stark, raised a hand to Andy and called, "Don't you worry, boy! We'll get this sorted out just as quick as winking!"

Fiz whispered, "That's what I'm scared of!" but Andy nudged her to keep quiet as Dad waved the last car off and came back to the house.

"Right." He sounded grim but satisfied. "It's all set. We'll be off at first light tomorrow – six of us, with guns and dogs. And we won't come back till we've found that brute, and dealt with it!"

He walked past them and indoors. Andy and Fiz stood staring after him, but they didn't speak. There was nothing to say.

In the house, Mum had kept Dad and Martin's dinners warm, and Dad switched on the TV as they sat down to eat. He'd missed the main news, but the local bulletin had just started.

And there on the screen, presenting the main item, was Kristie Kerr.

At first, Andy couldn't quite take in what the reporter was saying. He simply didn't believe it. But then he looked at Fiz's face. Saw her expression. Horror. Shame. *Guilt*.

". . . and this new development is sure to have animal welfare organizations in a ferment," said Kristie in melodramatic tones. "Some people, of course, agree that the big cat *should* be shot, before it can kill again. But we ask: is it *right* to kill a rare and beautiful animal out of hand, without making any attempt to capture it alive? The farmers of Fossewell certainly seem to think so. And now we have been told in confidence that they could be preparing to take the law into their own hands."

Andy didn't dare look at Dad, but he could hear him breathing. It sounded like a volcano that was about to erupt. . .

Kristie Kerr leaned confidentially towards the camera. "We'll be asking the views of the police and RSPCA, as well as talking with a spokesperson from one of the major animal welfare groups," she continued. "And of course we'd very much like to interview the Fossewell farmers. But whether they'll be as willing to talk to us . . . well, if there is, as we suspect, a conspiracy of silence, then the answer might be 'no'. This is Kristie Kerr, for DalesData, in Fossewell."

Dad exploded out of his chair. He was across the room in three strides and reaching for the phone. With a rage nearly as powerful bubbling up inside him, Andy turned on Fiz.

But Fiz wasn't there any more.

Martin was still staring at the TV, eyes goggling and mouth working. "How the hell did they find out?" he spluttered. "Who told them?"

Andy knew the answer as surely as if it had been written in fluorescent, metre-high letters on the wall. Fiz's face had given the whole game away. She'd lied to him. She'd cheated.

She'd told Kristie Kerr *everything*.

In the hall, Dad was ranting on the phone. Andy didn't know who he was talking to, and Dad ignored him as he squeezed past and ran up the stairs.

Fiz's bedroom door was shut, and when he tried the handle, it was locked, too. "Fiz!" He thumped with a clenched fist. "*Fiz!* Open this door!"

"Go away," came a muffled voice from the other side.

"No chance!" said Andy savagely. "I'm staying right here till you have the guts to face me!"

There was a long silence. When he pressed his ear to the door Andy thought he heard sniffling. Crying, was she? Served her right!

"Come on!" he said impatiently. "Open up."

There were some shufflings, then footsteps, then the door opened a fraction and Fiz's tear-streaked face looked out. She didn't say anything, and Andy felt disgusted.

"Well?" he demanded. Fiz looked away and he went on, "It was you, wasn't it? You told her!"

Fiz's expression crumpled. "She said she wouldn't use it. She promised me!"

"And you were dumb enough to believe her? I'd have thought even you had more sense than that!"

"She said she'd help!" Fiz wailed. "She said she loved animals, and didn't want to see it killed, and – and she knew someone who'd—"

"Oh, I bet she knows loads of people!" Andy interrupted ferociously. "Like TV producers, and newspaper editors – just the sort of people who'll pay her pots of money for a great scoop!" He sucked in a huge breath. "You just went ahead and blabbed, after all we'd said!"

Fiz really was crying again. "You don't understand," she said tragically. "I was scared, Andy! When we heard that shot, and you collapsed, I thought something awful had happened! And even when I knew it hadn't, I thought: what if it *is* real next time? What if the animal gets shot, and you – you –" She sniffed loudly. "She knew something was wrong, and she was so kind. . ."

"So you've told her everything I told you!"

"*No!* I didn't tell her everything! Only about the creature, and that we'd seen it, and knew what it was, and didn't want it to be killed!"

110

"I don't believe you!"

"But it's true!" Fiz pleaded. "I had to find a way to help you, and it seemed the only – the only – oh, what does it matter?" Suddenly, with a strength that surprised Andy, she wrenched the door handle out of his grasp, and slammed the door in his face.

"Fiz!" He hammered on the wood. "*Fiz!*"

This time, though, she wasn't going to open it. Seething, Andy put his mouth to the door and called through.

"You wait till I tell Dad. You just wait!" He didn't think about his next words; he was so angry that he just wanted to pay her back by scaring her. "You'll be lucky if he doesn't shoot *you!*" he finished, and stomped away to his own room.

Fiz sat shaking on her bed, staring at the door through a blur of tears. She didn't move for a long time. She could hear raised voices downstairs that sounded like people having some kind of argument, though she couldn't make out what was being said. Andy's parting threat went round and round in her mind. Would he tell on her? Fiz didn't know. If he did, Uncle Phil wouldn't shoot her; of course he wouldn't. But he'd be so furious that she'd probably rather be shot than face him. She couldn't bear that. She couldn't take it. She didn't have enough courage.

Her suitcase was standing in one corner of the room, and next to it was a good-sized shoulder bag. Fiz looked at them both. The suitcase was too big and heavy, she thought. But the bag. . . She could get the stuff she really needed in there, and the rest – well, right now she didn't care if she never saw it again.

She got to her feet, picked the bag up, and started to shove clothes haphazardly into it.

12

Andy was out in the woods. He knew instantly that this wasn't a dream, because he could see perfectly well in the dark and the ground was a lot closer than usual. He was sharing the big cat's mind again. He *was* the Fossewell Fiend.

His stomach wasn't gnawing, though, the way it had done before. He'd eaten well, and the memory of the last hunt started to creep into his thoughts. It had been a—

No! said the Andy part of him quickly. *I don't want to think about that!* He pushed it away, feeling queasy, and tried to concentrate on what was happening now. He'd been asleep, he thought, and something had

113

disturbed him. So he was moving slowly, silently through the trees, going to investigate.

He sniffed at the air, catching all sorts of scents that a human couldn't detect. Then one scent in particular alerted him. He knew it, and he didn't like it. He was afraid of it, because it was the scent of his enemies.

It was the scent of *them*.

His hackles came up, and he dropped to the ground, slithering forward until he reached the edge of the trees. He could see a field, with a footpath crossing it. There was one of *them* on the footpath, blundering along in the dark and carrying something on its back. He hissed softly. Only one. One alone wasn't a threat to him . . . and he was curious.

He started to move along the edge of the wood, keeping pace with the stumbling human. He was quite interested in it now. It wasn't very big, and its head looked unusually pale.

Pale. . .

Short blonde hair. . .

The Andy part of the two muddled minds felt a jolt of sheer horror as he realized the truth. It wasn't possible, it couldn't be happening – but it was!

Fiz. . .

Andy woke up with a shocked yelp, to find himself in his own bed. The mental link was gone, but he remembered every detail. And he knew what he'd seen out there in the woods!

"Oh, God!" He leaped out of bed and ran out to the landing. To Fiz's room.

"*Fiz? Fiz!*" He was whispering, then realized that if she was there, and asleep, she couldn't possibly hear him. He tried the door.

It wasn't locked any more.

Andy barged into the room and slammed the light on.

There was an empty bed, a suitcase, and fewer clothes lying around than there'd been yesterday. Fiz had gone.

Andy's heart started to pound. He knew where Fiz was. He'd seen her with his own eyes – or rather, with something else's eyes – not two minutes ago. She was out there in the night, alone. She was running away because of what had happened, and what he'd said.

Running into terrible danger. . .

He didn't stop to reason what he should do. Racing back to his room, he flung on clothes and trainers. There was a first glimmer of dawn in the sky, but it was still pretty dark, and he grabbed a torch before hurrying downstairs.

Mustn't wake anyone. They wouldn't believe that he knew where she was, and they'd waste hours looking in all the wrong places. He had to find her himself. . .

Meg jumped to her feet, tail wagging eagerly, as he burst into the kitchen. Andy hesitated a moment, then an idea came to him. He ran back to Fiz's room, grabbed her slippers (which she'd left behind), and dashed down again. Clipping the collie's lead on, he took her out to the yard and held the slippers under her twitching nose. "Meg! Find Fiz!"

Meg waved her tail, tried to chew one of the slippers – then suddenly she put her nose to the ground and started casting about.

"Good girl!" Andy encouraged her. "Find! Find Fiz!"

Meg yelped excitedly, and took off towards the field gate, towing Andy behind her. There was a bit of a muddle at the gate as the collie tried to dive underneath and had to be hauled back while Andy climbed over. But she picked up the scent on the other side, and they were off again.

After five minutes of stumbling after the excited dog, Andy realized that he'd made a big mistake. Meg was zigzagging around all over the place. She kept losing the scent, then she'd find it again – or seem to – and tear off in a new direction. Fiz wouldn't have done that. She would have headed in a fairly straight line, probably along the main path. But the path forked a bit further on. Which way had she gone then?

Andy stopped, hauling Meg back. If only he knew where the big cat had been when their minds were linked! He'd sort of recognized it, but it could have been any one of several places, miles apart. What was he going to do?

Meg was getting impatient. She wanted to carry on with this new game, and suddenly she decided to tell Andy so by barking loudly.

"Meg! Shut up!" Andy hissed urgently.

And from the yard a voice shouted, "Who's that? Who's out there?"

Andy looked back. There were lights in the house – and in the growing dawn he could make out the figure of Dad standing in the yard.

"Andy?" Dad had spotted him. "What the heck are you doing?"

Andy groaned inwardly. There was only one thing he could do. He had to tell the truth.

"Dad!" He ran back to the gate, Meg bounding beside him. "Oh, Dad – Fiz has run away! And it's all my fault."

"It *was* my fault," Andy said miserably. "I was so livid with her, I just said the most horrible things that came into my head. And the last thing – about Dad shooting her—"

"Now, stop being silly, Andy," Mum soothed. "She wouldn't have believed for a moment that he would."

"But the rest of it—"

"All right; maybe you upset her, and that's why she went. But she's a sensible girl. The likeliest thing is that she's planning to catch a train back to her school. She's got a return ticket, after all. The first bus from the village doesn't go for another hour, so she'll still be waiting at the stop."

Andy nodded. Martin had driven off to the bus stop to look for Fiz. He should be back soon, and then they'd know.

But he had a horrible feeling that Fiz wouldn't be there.

He was right. Martin returned ten minutes later, with the news that there was no sign of Fiz anywhere in the village.

"Where *is* she?" Andy asked desperately. Then he swallowed, hard. This had to be said. There was no other choice.

"Dad . . . I think she's . . . out in the country-side somewhere." Another swallow. "She might have tried to take the short cut over the fields, and – and got lost. And I keep thinking. . ."

He didn't need to say any more, because Dad, Mum and Martin all saw what he was getting at. Mum said softly, "Oh, no. . ."

"The cat. . ." Martin breathed. "It wouldn't attack a . . . a *person*. . .?"

"Wouldn't it?" Dad's face was grim. He looked at Martin, then at Mum. "All right. There's only one thing we can do." He swung round towards the hall. "I'm phoning the police!"

13

Within two hours, the farm was in turmoil. There were three police cars and a dog van in the yard, other farmers from around the district were turning up, and the house was full of people, including more than a dozen officers in uniform and plain clothes.

Andy had been questioned until his head spun. They'd urged him to tell every tiny detail he could remember, in case anything should give them a clue to where Fiz could have gone. The worst of it was, though, that Andy couldn't tell them the one thing that might have helped. If he could simply have said, "I saw her on the edge of some woods just before dawn," then this whole nightmare might quickly be over. But how could he? He wouldn't be believed, and they'd bust him for wasting police time, or something. All he could do – and had done – was tell them that Fiz had particularly liked the wooded country. At least it was *some* sort of a clue.

He hadn't been allowed to join the search parties. Dad and Martin had gone, and several other farmers, because they knew the country better than anyone. But they'd told him he was too young and would only get in the way. He'd tried, once, to sneak out of the yard and go off on his own, but Mum had spotted him and made him come back. At length he retreated to his room, feeling frustrated, and queasy with worry. If only he could help! If only he could have told the whole truth to someone who'd believe him!

There was the sound of an engine in the yard, and he looked out to see that a new vehicle had arrived. A large, heavy van, with no side windows and no markings. . . Frowning, Andy leaned out for a better look.

The van doors opened and several men climbed out. They were wearing heavy clothes and camouflage jackets, and they were carrying rifles.

Queasiness became a horrible, sick lurch, and Andy raced downstairs.

"Mum! Mum, there's—" He stopped as he came face to face with two of the men. They saw his eyes widen, and one of them smiled a friendly smile.

"Nothing to be scared of, lad – it's not you we're after!"

Andy started to tremble. "You – you're—"

"Police special team. We're going after the cat."

Horror hit Andy. He opened his mouth to shout, "No!" but then shut it, fast. He should have realized this was going to happen. It was so howlingly obvious. They were thinking of the danger to Fiz; they wouldn't worry about anything else. They didn't *know*. . .

"What are you – I mean, how –" But he couldn't get the words out properly.

"Oh, we'll get it, don't worry." The marksman smiled at him again, reassuringly. "Your cousin'll be all right. I'm sure she will."

Andy hoped and prayed she would. But what about him?

The most senior officer, who'd set up a temporary HQ in the sitting room, came out then to give the men their instructions. In another couple of minutes they were heading out of the yard. Andy stared blindly after them, watching until they were almost out of sight across the fields. He'd gone past being afraid. He was helpless, and a hideous sense of inevitability was growing inside him. Those men were trained. They were experts. They'd find the big cat, and they'd shoot it.

And when they did, Andy was sure that he, too, would die.

He was still standing numbly where he was when he heard the sound of yet more engines. His brain said dully, *Getting like a rush-hour motorway round here*, and he looked, though without any real interest, to see who else was coming to add to the chaos.

An outside broadcast van with the DalesData logo on it came swinging through the gate. And behind it was a yellow sports car.

Andy stared as Kristie Kerr jumped out. He didn't move as she hurried towards him with a broad smile on her face, and he didn't take the hand she offered him to shake. He only went on staring.

"Andy?" said Kristie, frowning with surprise. "It – er – is Andy, isn't it. . .?"

Andy blinked. He didn't even feel angry any

more. He just wanted her to know what she'd done.

He said in a flat, desolate voice, "This is all your fault."

"Now please, Mrs Thorpe, be reasonable!" Kristie was backing away from the house door, hands outspread, trying to make peace. "My job is to report the news, and you can't deny that a missing child is *major* news! We want to help! All I'm asking for is a description – a photo maybe—"

Mum's angry voice cut her off. "I don't care what you want! You've caused enough trouble already, and I don't believe a word you say! Just go away!"

The door slammed furiously, sending Kristie reeling back. The TV cameraman behind her shrugged and grinned wryly, but Kristie ignored him and stalked off towards her car, which she'd parked by the barn door.

As she reached it, Andy stepped out of the shadows.

Kristie stopped, and they looked at each other. Then, praying that Mum wasn't watching from the kitchen window, Andy said: "I know where the big cat's hiding. But if I tell

124

you, you've got to do something for me in return."

The thought had come to him like a cartoon light bulb popping into life in his head. All right: it *was* largely Kristie Kerr's fault that all this had happened. But he'd been partly to blame as well, for blowing up at Fiz just because she'd fallen for the reporter's ruse. Now Fiz was in danger, and so was he. The one chance they had was if the big cat could be caught rather than killed. The police wouldn't even consider that idea – as far as they were concerned, the animal had to be shot before it could attack again. It was a matter of life or death.

But it was also a matter of life or death to Andy. And Kristie Kerr was the only hope he had left.

He beckoned her into the barn, where no one would see them. Kristie's eyes were eager. "Andy," she said, "if you know where the Fossewell Fiend is—"

"I do," Andy interrupted. "But I'm not going to tell you until you've done your bit."

She nibbled her lip. "Which is. . .?"

"I want it to be caught alive. Never mind why, but it's desperately important to me.

Fiz said you know people. Experts."

Kristie nodded. "A good friend of mine's the big cat ranger at Redmoor Park."

Redmoor was a wild animal sanctuary, and a good one. Andy had been there several times.

"Good," he said. "Then I want you to phone him, and get him out here to catch it."

He could see her mind working behind the thoughtful look in her eyes. "And if I do," she said at length, "what do I get in return?"

"I'll tell them exactly where to look for it. And I'll be right."

"Hang on," said Kristie. "How do you know you'll be right?"

"I *do* know," Andy insisted. "But if I told you how, you wouldn't believe me. You'll just have to trust me."

Kristie thought about that for a moment, her eyes narrowing. "And you haven't told the police? They won't get there first?"

I hope to God they won't! Andy thought. Aloud, he said, "I haven't told anyone else. Because they wouldn't believe how I know, either."

"All right!" Excitedly, Kristie pulled out a mobile phone. "Now, where's Redmoor's number. . ." She punched buttons. "Ah! Got it." The mobile started to bleep. "Hello? Hello, Redmoor Park? This is Kristie Kerr, from DalesData. I need to speak to Ian Parsons – and it's urgent!"

"Stop there," said Andy. "It's as close as we can get."

Kristie nodded, and the sports car halted by the humpback bridge. They got out, and Andy pointed along the river.

"If we walk up there, we should meet your friends on the other side of the hill."

"Right." Kristie started to scramble down the bank. "Come on, then!"

They set off at a jog along the top of the sloping river bank. Andy's heart was bumping in time with his footsteps, and all he could think was: *They're coming. They're really coming!* A team from Redmoor Park, led by their big cat expert, with all the equipment they'd need to capture the creature alive. Andy could hardly believe that they'd acted so fast, but Kristie, it seemed, had influence. Andy realized, now, that she really *was* on his side. What she'd said to Fiz about being an animal lover was true – and a live cat would also make a wonderful "human interest" story for her programme. There was still the fear that the marksmen would find the cat before the wildlife team could. But at least now it – and Andy – had a chance.

The team were going straight out to the woods. It saved time, and it also avoided the almighty row that would have happened if they'd turned up at the farm. Andy had managed to sneak into Kristie's car when no one was looking, and in a few minutes they'd join up with the cat-catchers.

To Andy's relief, Kristie was as fit as he was, and they kept up a good pace along the bank. Then, as they got near the crest of the hill, Andy suddenly stopped, doubling over and clutching his head.

"Andy?" Kristie slid to a halt. "You OK?"

"N . . . no . . . oww, my *head*!" The pain had come surging back, and Andy's skull was throbbing agonizingly. The ground seemed to lurch; the scene around him spun.

Frightened! Angry!

The feelings slammed into his mind, and in the same instant he saw the world through the big cat's eyes. He was deep in among a thicket of trees, hidden as far as he could be from *them*. But though he'd thought he was safe, one of *them* had found him.

He knew where the human was. Like him, it was lying among the trees. It had been there for some time, and it didn't show any signs of going away. He wasn't curious about it now. He was angry. He wanted it to go away. This was his territory.

But it wouldn't go. So he would deal with it. He would make sure that it couldn't try to hurt him, ever again.

Ever again.

Andy felt the careful, powerful glide of the cat's muscular body as it crept forward. He saw the trees opening out, the steep, upward slope of the ground. . . There *was* someone there. Whoever it was, was huddled on the slope with its back propped against a tree trunk. One leg was hunched up, while the other was stretched out straight, as if it hurt. The person had jeans and an anorak on. Andy had seen that anorak before.

It was Fiz.

She didn't know the cat was approaching. She just sat there like a sack of potatoes, doing nothing. Andy screamed silently, *Fiz! Run, you idiot, RUN!* but of course she couldn't hear him. Then Fiz reached out, took hold of her outstretched leg and awkwardly, painfully, moved it a few centimetres, and he realized that she *couldn't* run. She'd hurt herself – twisted her ankle, maybe even broken it. She couldn't move at all.

And the big cat was creeping slowly, surely, up on her.

"*Aah!*" The link snapped, and suddenly Andy was himself again, standing on the river bank with Kristie staring at him in confusion.

"Andy, what—" she began.

Andy's face was horrified. In the brief moments of the mind-link, he'd recognized the spot where Fiz was stuck. And in a very few minutes, the cat was going to attack her.

"The team –" he gasped. "They're going to the wrong place!"

"*What?*" Kristie would have asked questions, but he didn't give her the chance.

"Go and find them – hurry! Tell them to come to the steep slope – the scarp – on the other side of the Ridge! I'll meet you there!"

Kristie yelled, "Andy!" but he'd already turned and was scrambling down the river bank. She made to run after him – then recalled the look on his face. He knew what was happening. Somehow, he *knew*.

And intuition told her to believe him.

She sprinted away along the path.

14

Where are you? Andy sent the frantic mental message again, shutting his eyes tightly in an effort to concentrate. *Link with me again! Oh please, you've got to hear me! You've got to feel my thoughts!*

Nothing. The pain had gone, and the only mind inside his head was his own.

At least he knew where to look for the cat. But however fast he ran, whatever short cuts he took, splashing through the river, ripping his clothes on gorse or brambles, there was so little time! Right at this moment the animal could be slinking the last few metres towards Fiz; tensing, crouching, about to spring—

"*No!*" He shouted it aloud, despairingly, though it did no good because there was no one to hear him. Or – or would the cat hear? Would the sound of a voice distract it, and give him another vital minute?

He opened his mouth to yell again – and choked the cry back as, in the distance, he saw about a dozen men in dark clothes. They were moving steadily and purposefully, in a wide-spread line, towards the gentler slope of the Ridge. And Andy's eyes were sharp enough to see that they had guns.

"Oh, no!" He dared not shout again, not now. If the marksmen heard him, they'd come running! Sucking breath into his aching lungs, Andy ducked as low as he could, so the men wouldn't see him, and raced on. He was approaching the trees now; once he reached them he'd have to struggle through about a hundred metres of woodland before he got to the top of the slope.

Don't hurt Fiz! he prayed. *Don't, don't, please don't!* If only he could make contact with the cat! He'd never been able to control the mind-link; it happened randomly. But if this once, just this once –

He had to concentrate on other things then,

as he came up to the trees and plunged in among them. The going was much harder; branches whipped across his face and the ground was treacherous with hidden holes and protruding roots. *Mustn't make Fiz's mistake. Mustn't fall and sprain something.* On he went, stumbling and scrambling. Birds squawked in alarm, flurrying in the trees overhead. The cat would notice that. The birds might divert it from Fiz. Oh, they must!

Andy came to the top of the steep slope so suddenly that he almost pitched over the edge before he could stop himself. A wild grab at a tree trunk saved him, and he clung on, gasping for breath and peering down into the tangle of vegetation that fell away in front of him. No sign of any movement. Could he risk calling out? Better not. If Fiz heard him, she'd shout back, and what might the cat do then?

He started to slither down the slope, going carefully, grasping at branches to lessen the risk of a headlong fall. Far down, now, he could see the glitter of the river where it curved round the foot of the scarp. Not far to go, then. *If* he was right. . .

He was making a lot of noise now. The trees rustled and creaked as he held them, and his feet dislodged stones and clods of earth that went bouncing away downhill. Couldn't be helped. He hoped Kristie had done what he wanted her to. He hoped the wildlife team were coming. He hoped they'd *hurry*.

Suddenly, a tussock that he'd just trodden on gave way. Andy lost his footing and fell. He landed with a whack on his backside, and next instant he was sliding down the slope, as if he was on a fairground helter-skelter. He grabbed for branches but missed; he was going faster and faster – then a big tree loomed up ahead, and his feet slammed against it, stopping him with a teeth-rattling jolt.

He was winded and would have a few bruises tomorrow, but that was all. Relieved, he waited half a minute until he had enough breath to move, then started to climb to his feet.

And stopped dead.

Five metres away, crouched and motionless, was the cat. Its camouflage was so good that it had been completely invisible until this moment. But now its green-gold eyes were glaring at Andy, and as he stared, stunned, it drew its lips back slowly in a silent, menacing display.

Just a few paces beyond the cat was Fiz.

Fiz had seen Andy – but she'd also seen the

animal. Her eyes were blank with terror, and even from here Andy could see that she was shaking uncontrollably. He wanted to call out to her, tell her to keep absolutely still and not, *not* make a sound. But he couldn't risk it. At the slightest provocation the cat might attack either of them. . .

It was *huge*. Bigger than he'd realized. Not a leopard; no way. He knew, now, what it must be. A jaguar. Third biggest of all the cats, and a deadly predator. A wild part of his mind that didn't seem to belong to him said, *It's so beautiful!* But he couldn't think of that: couldn't think of anything except the danger that he and Fiz were in. One swipe of a massive paw, one bite, could kill either of them.

The jaguar was still staring at Andy. Then its long tail twitched. The movement made him jump; instantly the animal's ears went back and it growled – and Fiz's voice rose in a panicky wail.

"O-o-oh, And-yy—"

Like lightning, the jaguar whirled towards her. Andy knew what was going to happen, and there wasn't time to think rationally. He screamed, with all the strength he had, *"NO!"*

and at the same moment his mind hurled a desperate message, willing the great cat to hear and understand.

Don't hurt her! Don't, don't, DON'T!

The jaguar froze in mid-movement, and its head swung until it was looking at him again. And suddenly a new picture came into Andy's head. It was like double vision – he saw the cat, crouching, uncertain. And he saw himself from its viewpoint, half on his feet, wide-eyed. It was a dizzying experience – but for the first time Andy believed he could keep a grip on his own mind without losing the link. The jaguar's thoughts were ragged and confused, and he realized that in its own way it was as frightened as he and Fiz were. It didn't want to harm them. It only wanted to be left alone.

We can't leave you alone, Andy told it. *If we do, someone else will find you, and hurt you. We want to help you. Please, let us help you. . .*

It didn't understand words, of course, but he tried to show it what he meant. Kind thoughts. Encouraging thoughts. *Friends. Not enemies – friends.* Over and over again he projected it. And slowly, gradually, he began to feel the jaguar's mind responding. It didn't *exactly* trust him, but it sensed that he didn't want to hurt it, the way the *others* did. It was a start. Now, the next thing Andy had to do was persuade it to follow him when he moved very slowly away. Follow, but not attack.

He waved to Fiz, signalling her to keep as still and quiet as she possibly could. The jaguar's ears pricked forward again and, hoping Fiz had got the message, Andy rose cautiously to his feet.

He felt the flash of alarm in the cat's mind, the sudden doubt followed by a flicker of aggression. *No*, he projected. *No harm. Friend.*

He started to back away. This wasn't going to be easy. He didn't want to take his eyes off the jaguar, in case that broke the link, so he couldn't look where he was going. But he had to lead it away from Fiz and along the side of the hill, to the place where he'd told Kristie to bring the wildlife people. They should be there by now. They should be ready. . .

The jaguar looked at Fiz, and Andy felt the flicker of aggression again. *No*, he told the mind that tangled with his. *Mustn't hurt. Mustn't attack. No.*

It hesitated. Then, to his enormous relief,

the angry feeling faded and it followed him. It was still very wary, and Andy was uncomfortably aware that at any moment it might change its mind and decide he was an enemy after all. *Don't think about that,* he told himself. *Just keep going. . .*

He began to edge downhill, moving slantwise on the slope. The jaguar turned too, moving much more smoothly than he could. This was tricky. One wrong step and he could go hurtling down that hill like a kicked football. *Slowly, Andy,* he told himself. *No need to rush.*

Then from somewhere below came a shrill shout. "Andy! Are you up there?"

It was Kristie's voice, and it was so unexpected that Andy started violently. The jaguar started, too. Its head turned. It snarled — then the snarl turned into a full-throated roar, and it swung around and charged away down the slope.

"Oh, NO!" Andy scrabbled to regain his footing. "Come back! *Come back!*"

The cat ignored him, and his head spun dizzily as, again, he saw the scene through both pairs of eyes at the same time. One picture was like a crazy kaleidoscope, swaying and zigzagging madly as the jaguar leaped from one foothold to the next. The other was a distant view of the cat itself, gaining speed. Then he was the jaguar again, and there were people ahead of him. He was charging straight for them; he was roaring; he was going to *attack*—

"*Look out!*" Andy screamed. Without a single thought for his own safety, he launched himself down the slope and plunged after the jaguar. For a few astonishing, giddying seconds he kept his balance, running and jumping as the cat had done. Then—

"AAAH!" The world turned upside down and Andy pitched helplessly forward into what felt like empty space. It wasn't empty for long. He hit the ground, hard, and started to roll and tumble down the hill. Stones showered on him, bushes whanged him – there was a noise like thunder in his head, and somewhere people were shouting and someone – him? – screaming.

And he was the jaguar, and they were his enemies, and his muscles bunched for the final, powering rush—

Andy, still rolling, saw the huge, protruding tree root speeding to meet him, but there wasn't a thing he could do about it. In the instant before impact he glimpsed something else – a rushing shape, a spotted coat, the dark flicker of something whirling outwards. He felt a surge of shock and fear and fury that had nothing to do with his real self –

Then he slammed headlong into the root, and after that he didn't feel anything else at all.

15

When he came round, someone was dabbing the side of his head with a damp cloth.

"OK, OK, take it slowly!" said a voice as Andy tried to sit up in a rush. "How're you feeling?"

Good question. Andy's head hurt, but not in the way it did when the headaches came. This pain was much more real.

He looked at his rescuer, who was a youngish man with ginger hair and beard. "Hi," the man said with a smile. "I'm Ian Parsons. And you, I presume, are Andy?"

"Y . . . yeah. . ." He winced, and Ian's smile became a grin.

"You're going to have a pretty spectacular bruise there, but I don't think there's any other real damage."

Damage. . . "Fiz!" Andy said in alarm, remembering.

"She's fine. They're bringing her down now. She twisted her ankle, but apart from that she was as lucky as you. Good thing it wasn't too cold last night, eh?"

There was something else he should ask about, Andy thought. His head was muzzy, but he *knew* there was something else. . .

Then he heard a soft noise, like a very large person sighing.

He whipped round so quickly that it set his head thumping again. "*Oww*. . ." He shut his eyes until the pain faded a bit, then, more carefully, looked.

Ian saw his expression and said quietly, "He's a beauty, isn't he?"

The jaguar was lying in the grass a few metres from the river bank. It was tangled in the folds of a net, but it wasn't struggling; it simply lay on its side, eyes half closed. It looked strangely peaceful.

"You . . . you got him. . ." Andy said wonderingly.

Ian nodded. "We did – thanks to you. He's a bit sleepy now, because we've given him a sedative. But he's OK. And the most important thing is, he's safe. No one's ever going to go after him with a gun again."

Footsteps rustled, and Kristie came over from where she'd been talking to one of the other trappers. "They've got the cage ready, Ian," she said. "So if – Andy! Hey, you're awake!"

"Yeah," said Andy. "Sort of. . ."

Kristie dropped to a crouch beside him. "You were brilliant! Getting that huge cat to run straight into the net – how did you do it?"

Was that what had happened? Andy couldn't remember. All he recalled was sending one final plea to the jaguar as he hurtled towards the tree root that had knocked him out. He'd tried to tell it, *We only want to help you. . .* And then the world had blanked out.

Well, maybe the jaguar had understood. He'd still been linked to it at that moment, seeing what it saw, feeling what it felt. Maybe, somehow, he'd had an effect on it, and that was why it had allowed itself to be caught. . . It wasn't very likely. But then, the idea of being linked to an animal's mind wasn't exactly believable either, was it? Yet it had happened. *It had happened.*

He looked at the great cat again. It wasn't really asleep. Its eyes were still half open, and as their gazes met, Andy realized something. The link was broken. Not in the way it had been broken before – this time, it had truly gone. He didn't know how he could be so sure, but he was, and gently he felt his skull. Funny – the root had whanged him on the same spot as the table, when he'd fallen out of bed after that first weird dream. It was a coincidence, of course. Had to be. But all the same . . . could there be a connection with the mingling of minds?

He'd never know the answer for sure. But he knew what he believed.

Kristie's voice broke into his thoughts. "We've got two four-wheel drives here, so Ian's taking the cat back to Redmoor, and you and Fiz are going to hospital in the other car."

Andy nodded. "Thanks. I – suppose someone'll have to tell Mum and Dad. And the police." He shivered. "They'll have my guts on a plate when they find out what I did. . ."

"They will not!" said Kristie firmly. "The only thing they'll really care about is that you and

Fiz are all right. You leave them to me, and if there is any flak, I'll take it." She laughed. "It's well worth it, for the story I'm going to get!"

New voices came echoing out of the trees then, saying things like, "Left a bit!" and "Watch out for her other leg!" and two men appeared, carrying Fiz between them. She looked tired and dishevelled and very pale, but she managed to grin at Andy and wave a hand.

"Hiya," she said weakly, then: "Whoo!"

That just about summed it up, Andy thought. There was tons more to say, but it'd keep.

He grinned back. "Come on," he replied. "You're keeping everyone waiting – I want my free ride in a swanky new four-wheel drive!"

"So how does it feel to be famous?" Fiz turned away from the enclosure gates and looked solemnly at Andy.

He shrugged. "Dunno, really. Sort of . . . uncomfortable. But nice in a way, too. Specially when you think about the reason."

"Mmm. I think I feel the same."

They had just finished their interview with Kristie Kerr, and the thought that, tonight, they'd see themselves on DalesData's local news broadcast was more than a little weird.

But, as Andy said, the reason for their fame was enough to make them feel good.

It had been a hectic week, to put it mildly. First there'd been all the fuss at the hospital, with Mum, Dad, Martin, police, journalists and God alone knew who else adding to the chaos. Then, when Andy and Fiz were pronounced OK and allowed to go home, there'd been the questions to answer. What had happened. Why it had happened. What they had done. Kristie Kerr had been as good as her word, insisting that she was the one who'd called in the wildlife team. The police hadn't been too pleased about her going behind their backs, but they weren't going to take things any further. No one had come to any real harm, and that was what counted.

When Andy had tried to apologize to Fiz, she'd told him not to be an idiot. If she was dumb enough to go stomping off in a huff in the small hours of the morning, she'd said, then she only had herself to blame for the trouble that followed. As Andy had already guessed, she'd been heading for the village, taken what she though was a short cut, and got completely lost. Then, in the dark, she'd tripped and twisted her ankle. She'd managed to get some way up the slope after it happened, but eventually it was just too painful, so she'd fallen asleep where she was and . . . well, Andy knew the rest, didn't he? Luckily she'd had warm clothes on, so she hadn't got hypothermia or anything.

"And anyway," she'd added, as Andy opened his mouth to say that he still felt guilty, "if it wasn't for me, you wouldn't have caught the jaguar, would you? So I'm the *real* hero!"

They looked back at the enclosure. They couldn't see the jaguar, but they knew it was there, in a clump of bushes near a specially built log shelter. Ian Parsons said that it usually slept during the day, preferring to come out and patrol its new territory at night. It was settling down well, he'd told them. And the best news of all was that, because it was young and healthy and obviously capable of looking after itself, they hoped that one day it could be taken to its natural home in South America and released into the wild.

They didn't know where the jaguar had come from, and probably never would. Ian's guess was that someone was probably keeping it illegally, and it had either escaped or deliberately been turned loose. No one, of course, would ever own up to being responsible. But for this cat, at least, the story had ended happily.

Andy was about to walk away when Fiz suddenly grasped his arm. "Look!" she said softly.

The jaguar had emerged from the bushes. It blinked in the sunlight – then it saw them. But it didn't snarl, or duck out of sight again. Instead, it strolled into the centre of its enclosure, then sat down and started to lick itself.

"He *is* beautiful!" Fiz whispered. "I'm so glad he didn't die."

"So am I." Andy smiled at her. "Hey – I've had an idea. If he *is* released one day . . . well, your parents spend a lot of time in South America, don't they?"

"Yeah."

"So what're the chances of us wangling a trip with them, to see him set free?"

She laughed. "Brilliant! I'll talk them into it. Blackmail them, if I have to! Start practising your Spanish, Andy Thorpe!"

Andy looked back at the jaguar. It had stopped washing and was watching him. It looked very intent, and for a moment – just one – he thought he felt a faint little ache in his head, as if. . .

No. It was only his imagination. The link had served its purpose, but now it was gone for good. And that was probably just as well.

But all the same, as he turned away, it seemed to him that there was a message in the jaguar's eyes. Silent but clear, it seemed to say: *Goodbye, friend. Maybe I'll see you again, one day. . .*

Are they ordinary animals – or are they **Creatures**?

To find out about other **Creatures** titles by **Louise Cooper** turn the page and read on

Creatures

Give a Dog a Bone

Chris bit his lip, then his shoulders heaved. "OK. But it sounds totally stupid. There's Nathaniel's statue, right? And Lancer's next to him. Well, I could see them both clearly from my window."

He hesitated again, then with an effort turned to face Pippa. He looked embarrassed. And he also looked frightened.

"I wasn't dreaming," he said, "and I didn't imagine it. The moon was out and the statues had shadows. The statue of Lancer was completely still; I mean, it's made of stone, so of course it was. But . . ." He swallowed. "Honest, Pippa, I'm not joking. Lancer's shadow was *moving*."

Creatures

Atishoo! Atishoo! All Fall Down!

Turning away from the cage, Kel started to walk towards the door. The others followed.

And Chocky said, quite clearly, "Susie won't hurt *you*."

They all stopped dead. Turned. Stared. Birds can't grin, but if Chocky had been human there would have been a smirk on his face.

"Susie won't hurt *you*," he repeated, then paused as if he was thinking – or listening to something no one else could hear. "Susie *likes* you."

Creatures

Who's Been Sitting in My Chair?

"Opal!" Not knowing whether to feel relieved or annoyed, Rhoda started towards the armchair.

Then suddenly, in the cushioned depths of the chair's seat, a pair of eyes appeared.

There was nothing else. No face, no shape; just *eyes*. They were almond-shaped, amber-yellow, and had huge black pupils that glared furiously at Rhoda.

The purring stopped. There was an instant's absolute silence – then a piercing animal screech ripped through the room, an appalling din that battered Rhoda's ears. Her mouth opened in the beginnings of a terrified scream—

Creatures

See How They Run

He spun round. Behind him, on the floor, were six very large rats. They were sitting up on their haunches, front paws raised, staring at him.

Then he saw eight more in the doorway. These were smaller – more like normal size – but they were sitting up, too. Very still. Very quiet. *Staring*.

Jon swallowed. He moved the torch – and there were more rats, on a fallen beam that lay at a sloping angle between the ceiling and the floor. Lined in a row, sitting up, and absolutely motionless as they watched with their mean, beady little eyes.

The ugly truth dawned on Jon even before he started to swing the torch around in a wide arc. There were rats everywhere.

Creatures

If You Go Down
to the Woods

"It's gone!" Caroly whispered. Her face was dead white and she looked as if she was going to be sick. "But how? It can't have *walked*!"

"Can't it?" said Alex. The horrible thought she had had earlier was creeping back. The owl. The fox. The bag. All those tracks in the snow.

And Chaz. . .

"They're coming alive," she said in a small, fearful voice. "The animals in our props and costume bits . . . They're *all* coming alive!"